A warmth glowed deep inside, and she was reluctant to see the evening end. . . .

"Guess I'd better be going," Pete said as he rose from the couch. Vonnie followed him to the door and snapped on the porch light. But Pete reached up and snapped it off. Then he took her in his arms and kissed her slowly and tenderly—just the way she imagined it would be.

"Good night, Vonnie."

And he was gone before she could say a word.

Dear Reader,

At Silhouette we publish books with you in mind. We're pleased to announce the creation of Silhouette First Love, a new line of contemporary romances written by the finest young-adult writers as well as outstanding new authors in this field.

Silhouette First Love captures many of the same elements enjoyed by Silhouette Romance readers—love stories, happy endings and the same attention to detail and description. But First Love features young heroines and heroes in contemporary and recognizable situations.

You play an important part in our future plans for First Love. We welcome any suggestions of comments on our books and I invite you to write to us at the address below.

Jane Nicholls
Silhouette Books
PO Box 177
Dunton Green
Sevenoaks
Kent
TN13 2YE

SPECIAL GIRL
Dorothy Francis

First Love from Silhouette

Published by Silhouette Books

Copyright © 1981 by Dorothy B. Francis

First printing 1983

British Library C.I.P.

Francis, Dorothy
    Special girl.—(Silhouette first love)
    I. Title
    813'.54[F]   PS3556.R/

    ISBN 0 340 33678 1

Printed and bound in Great Britain for
Hodder and Stoughton Paperbacks, a
division of Hodder and Stoughton Ltd.,
Mill Road, Dunton Green, Sevenoaks,
Kent (Editorial Office: 47 Bedford
Square, London, WC1 3DP) by
Richard Clay (The Chaucer Press) Ltd.,
Bungay, Suffolk

For Ann

1

Vonnie Morrison was doing errands with her father that February afternoon when she first saw Pete Karmer. Of course she didn't know his name then. Nor was she very well acquainted with Roe Village. The small town consisted of small shops and businesses which lined the narrow streets around a central square and sunlight glazed the windows of a gray concrete and glass courthouse that dominated the square like the set in a ring.

It was Saturday and she and her father were shopping for a list of things jotted down on the back of an old envelope. Scouring powder. Oven cleaner. Detergent. They had purchased most of the items at the supermarket and now they were hunting for the Johnson Hardware Store. Whenever they moved, her father always found lots of things to repair and improve in their new house and this time was no exception.

She glanced at the list again. Sandpaper. Steel wool. Paint. Those things were written in her father's bold handwriting. She glanced at him and smiled as she realized that he matched his handwriting. Bold. He was so tall and big-boned and muscular that he had to scrunch down to fit in their compact car. And his features were bold too. His high broad forehead, prominent nose, square chin were barely softened by his thrush-colored hair and blue eyes. Baby blue, her mother called them when she wanted to tease him.

Vonnie's smile changed to a frown as they drove around a block. Her father worked for Eckert Electronics Corporation as a time study expert and he was good at his job. The company moved him to any plant that was having production problems and after a few months those problems usually cleared up under his supervision. She couldn't guess why he didn't apply his efficiency to his own life. Why hadn't he looked up the address of Johnson Hardware before they left home? It would have saved time and gas and . . .

"There it is, Dad." Vonnie pointed to a signboard on the corner to her right. "Johnson Hardware."

"See?" Dad said. "I told you we'd find it without any trouble. Roe Village just isn't big enough to lose a hardware store in."

Vonnie sighed and shook her head. They had only arrived in Roe Village, Kansas, yesterday and she was still so excited over the move that sometimes she smiled over things that might well have made her frown. This was the first time her family had moved to the Midwest. Always before they had lived in Washington or Oregon or Michigan or North Dakota. Lots of times when she was little she had hated to move and leave friends and favorite teachers behind, but when she had reached high school her life had changed. She didn't really regret leaving Utica, Washington. They had only lived there six months and she really hadn't made any close friends in her junior class. But her life in Roe Village was going to be different. She was going to conquer her shyness and make friends. She was going to be in clubs and organizations and she was going to be able to do those things because she was going to keep her secret from everyone. She was not going to let even one person know she was . . . different.

At first when her father had said they were moving to Roe Village she had been disappointed. Then she had learned that it was just a few miles from Kansas City. There would be lots of exciting things to do in the city and this time she was going to have friends to do those things with. It was just a matter of keeping her mouth shut.

Mr. Morrison opened his car door. "Vonnie, if you'll pick up the steel wool and the sandpaper, I'll talk to someone about mixing the paint. That'll save a little time. I'm eager to get back home."

"Sure, Dad." Vonnie sighed. "How can you think of that big old house as home so soon? I can't. Not yet, anyway."

Her dad grinned. "I liked our modern ranch-style house back in Washington, Vonnie, but here the only rental house available was the huge old Victorian."

"I'm glad it's just two blocks from the high school." Vonnie thought the place was fascinating with its gingerbread curlicues, its round tower on the west, its high ceilings. But so far the thing she liked best about it was its location near the school. She would be able to walk home for lunch and that would please her mother and be a strong arguing point when she told her folks she was going to keep her secret. She hadn't dared approach the subject yet, but she knew she would have to before she left for school on Monday morning.

As they entered the hardware store she inhaled the mingling odors of varnish, hemp rope and turpentine. She glanced at a man dressed in overalls topped with a green jacket and a billed seed-corn cap, who was looking at a bin of nails. Then she saw *him*. He was standing near the cash register writing up a sales ticket for a customer and she had a chance to study him for a few moments before he looked up and saw her. He was about her age, or he might even be a senior. Tall. Rangy. And he was wearing a blue and white gingham shirt and khaki work pants. His crisply curling dark hair was the color of ripe walnuts still in the hull and when he looked up at his customer Vonnie saw that he had the bluest eyes she had ever seen. Or maybe it was his blue shirt that made them seem so. He had a broad strong face and when he looked at her and smiled, a dimple appeared in his left cheek.

"May I help you?" he asked.

Suddenly Vonnie felt her mouth go dry and she tried to swallow. What was wrong with her! She had vowed that she was going to behave differently in this new town. Moving here was going to be the start of a new life and everything was going to be perfect. She wasn't going to be shy and scared and . . . but she was shy and scared and she didn't know what to say. No, that was wrong. Of course she knew what to say. She looked down at her shopping list.

"I need three sheets of sandpaper—fine—and a box of steel wool."

"I'll get them for you." The boy smiled again, walked to the display shelves to his left, then returned with the items and laid them on the counter beside the cash register. "Will that be all?"

Vonnie forced herself to stop staring at the boy's

strong square hands and met his gaze again. "No.
My father's in the back getting some paint." Vonnie
nodded to the rear of the store. "He may decide on
some more things before he leaves."

The boy smiled at her. "You must be new in town.
I don't remember seeing you around before."

"We just got here yesterday. At least I think we're
here. The moving van's gone and everything's in the
-house, but we're not unpacked yet. We're still living
out of boxes and barrels." She felt herself blushing.
She hadn't meant to go on and on as if she were the
only person in the world who had ever moved or
something. Their eyes met and she looked away,
embarrassed. She guessed he sensed her embarrass-
ment and wanted to put her at ease because he went
on talking.

"Where are you from?"

"Washington state." Her throat seemed to close
up and choke off more words. Where was all her
resolve to reach out, to make friends? That telephone commercial made reaching out seem a lot
easier than it really was.

"Washington," he repeated. "That's a long ways
from here."

"Yes." How inane could she sound!

"How'd you happen to land in Roe Village?"

"Dad's job brought us here. He's with Eckert
Electronics in the city."

"Going to commute, huh?"

She nodded, her mouth and throat so dry she was
about to choke.

"Lots of people commute to the city. Small town
living appeals to lots of families. Where will you be
living?"

Vonnie felt a pulse pounding at her temple. Could

11

he see it? He wanted to know where she lived. Or maybe he was just being polite. It was just small talk. Clerks had to be good at small talk. "We've rented that big old house on Elm Street . . . near the school."

"Oh, the old Williams place. I mean a family named Williams has owned the house for years. Sometimes I wish I lived that close to school. I could sleep a little later in the morning."

"Where do you live?" She blurted out the question and then wondered if he thought she was being too forward. Yet he had asked her where she lived, hadn't he?

"I live out on the old highway. Dad farms."

"And you don't like the country?"

"I like it okay, it's just that living in town would be a lot more convenient sometimes."

"I suppose so." Again she couldn't think of anything more to say and she just stood there wishing her father would hurry with the paint. Maybe she could go back and join him. She turned to leave just as the boy spoke again.

"What year are you in in school?"

"Junior."

"Hey, me too. We'll probably have some classes together."

Before Vonnie could comment, her father arrived with three cans of paint, some brushes and paint thinner, plunked them on the counter by the cash register and ended her conversation with the boy. Maybe they would have some classes together. Vonnie hoped so. Her father paid for the purchases, thanked the boy and turned to leave the store. Vonnie wished she could think of something else to say to him, something that would let him know she was friendly without being pushy, something that would let him know she wasn't a nerd. But she couldn't think of a thing. She picked up the sack with the sandpaper and steel wool and walked out of the store with her father.

"Nice looking boy," her father commented as they got back into the car. "What's his name?"

Vonnie felt her face grow hot. "I don't know. He didn't say." Why hadn't she asked him his name! That would have been a logical question: What's your name? But he hadn't asked hers either, so they were even there. She guessed he didn't care that much about knowing who she was. Suddenly she thought about her looks. Maybe she should think about doing something different with her hair. She was glad she had her dad's coloring—brown hair and blue eyes, but maybe she had outgrown the Dutch bob hairstyle. Maybe she should try a pixie cut like her mother's. Or maybe she should let her hair grow long and curl it or wear it pinned up some way. Or maybe it was her clothes that were wrong. Maybe he didn't like tall girls in jeans. But that was dumb. Everyone wore jeans. And she was only a little over five feet six.

"Well, you'll probably see him at school on Monday," her dad said. "Plenty of time to learn names."

If she had told him her name he probably would have told her his. Now it would be embarrassing if and when they met again at school and had to introduce themselves. She sighed. If she was going to make her life in Roe Village, Kansas, any different from her life in Utica, Washington, or Fargo, North Dakota, or Flint, Michigan, she was going to have to shape up. She was going to have to conquer her shyness. Or at least hide it. She had already decided that this move was going to mark a turning point in her life. No more feeling self-conscious. No more being the girl who was different. She would think of herself as the girl with a secret and maybe a certain mystique would shine through her smile and give her a fascinating personality.

She was dreaming. Who would ever find her fascinating!

2

She and her father didn't talk much as they drove through town. She was still thinking about the boy in the hardware store and wishing she had been sure of the right things to say to him, the things that would have made him eager to know her better. She had blown it again.

The February afternoon was golden with sunlight and the westerly breeze held just a hint of spring. Her father drove to a service station out on the highway to fill the gas tank and on the way back to their house they passed a semi-new housing development where the TV antennas were still taller than the trees. Then they reached the old section of town where they lived. Here oaks and maples lined the street, their leafless branches forming a dark lacework against the backdrop of sky.

The old house sat well back from the street and gnarled vines clinging to the white frame siding were like brown ropes holding the structure together. The green roof matched the green shutters and the green porch steps, and a red-brick chimney emitted white wisps of smoke into the air. The house had a homey, friendly look about it, Vonnie thought. Maybe when they got some curtains up at the windows . . . She opened the door and stepped inside.

"Welcome home," Vonnie's mother called, stepping from the kitchen into the dining room where she could see the front entryway. "Did you find everything on the list?" Loboy, their dachshund, came running to greet them too, sniffing at their shoes and muttering a half-bark deep in his throat.

"We found everything," her father answered.

Vonnie smiled at her mother's appearance. She usually wore an artist's smock over jeans, but today her petite form was hidden under one of her father's huge sweat shirts and she wore a red kerchief around her dark brown hair. The exertion of unpacking had made her cheeks rosier than usual and they seemed to bring out the green in her hazel eyes. Her mother had a way of looking at home no matter where she was.

Home. Would she ever be able to call this place home! She looked at the high tray ceilings, the old-fashioned chandelier with multi-colored glass and beaded fringe. And above the front door a fanlight of blue, scarlet and green glass filtered colored sunlight onto the polished oak floors. Their low sleek-lined furniture seemed at odds with the flowered wallpaper, the tall narrow windows. There was no front hall closet, so Vonnie carried her coat up to her bedroom. She wondered what *his* house was like.

"Want some hot chocolate?" her mother called to her from the bottom of the stairway.

"Later, Mom, but thanks. I need to start unpacking some more of these boxes."

"I'll leave it on the stove," her mother called back. "Help yourself when you're ready."

Vonnie looked around her room. She liked the sunny walls which were papered in yellow. Her bed and dresser and chest fitted into the room nicely and her white bedspread looked fine with the yellow walls. Right now there was nothing at the windows except the kind of shade you pulled down from a roller, but Mom had promised that she could choose fabric and make her own curtains just as soon as all the cartons and barrels were unpacked.

She pulled a box across the bare floor and began laying sweaters and underthings into the chest of drawers. Bare floor. She hated that, but her mother had promised her she could buy two small area rugs. She worked quickly, determined to get all her things in order today and tomorrow so her mind would be free to think about school and the people she would be meeting on Monday. Now the sun was setting, reminding her that February was a gloomy month and that starting in a new school was a gloomy prospect. But this time it was going to be different. She was going to make it different. . . .

"I know what lies ahead of me," she said to herself. "I've got to move slowly and cautiously and not come across as pushy." She knew that special interest groups and cliques would have been formed long ago and that to try to break into any of them right away would be foolhardy. She would have to be pleasant to everybody and to smile and smile and smile some more, and she would have to pretend that she didn't notice people whispering about her. New kids in school always got whispered about.

But there were advantages to moving into a new school too. Being the new girl in town wasn't all that bad. The kids might be whispering about her behind her back, but they would be noticing her. And this time it was going to be *different*. She was only going to let them notice the good things about her. No more medical bracelet. Before she had left Washington she had had the bracelet converted into a medallion she could wear around her *neck—under* her sweaters and shirts.

"Vonnie, supper's ready." Mother was calling to her again and she looked at her watch, not realizing how much time had passed. But she had accomplished a lot. She nested four empty cartons and carried them to the narrow stairway that led to the attic. Then she stopped in the bathroom, the worst room in the whole house. She had never seen a bathtub on legs before, nor had she ever seen a toilet that one flushed by pulling an overhead chain. Today she pulled that chain cautiously, but no matter how gently she or anyone else pulled it, the results were the same. As the toilet flushed, ancient pipes vibrated, making lots of thumping and bumping inside the ancient walls of the house. In a way it was funny and Vonnie ran downstairs to see the action.

Once the pipes stopped vibrating and wheezing there was a short silence, then everyone could hear mice scampering inside the old walls. This activity set Loboy into a frenzy of action and he ran down the hallway madly barking at the walls.

"People will think we have a psychotic dog," her father said, watching Loboy in action.

"We'll simply have to get rid of those mice." Her mother shuddered. "I'll call the exterminator first thing Monday."

"And we'll *never* flush the toilet if there's company in the house," Vonnie said. "That's gotta be a rule."

"Are you expecting company?" her father asked.

Vonnie felt herself blushing. "No, of course not, but sometimes you have business associates stop by . . . and . . ."

"The exterminators will take care of everything," her mother said. "Don't borrow trouble."

The kitchen had a breakfast alcove off one end with built-in benches and a formica-top table, and Vonnie slid onto the bench. Spaghetti and meatballs, garlic bread, tossed salad. It was her favorite meal to eat and her mother's favorite meal to prepare because she could make the meatballs and the sauce and let it simmer until mealtime. Her mother wasn't great on cooking. To prepare chicken and mashed potatoes on Sunday was a peak culinary accomplishment, but both Vonnie and her father liked to cook so there was no danger of starvation. They took turns in the kitchen.

"I've almost got the kitchen in order," Mrs. Morrison said. "And maybe you can help me unpack the good dishes after supper, Vonnie."

"Sure, Mom. Glad to."

"I'm getting a workshop sort of organized in the basement," Mr. Morrison commented. "We'll be settled in before we know it."

"Have you seen the attic?" Mother smiled at them. "It's going to make the *perfect* painting studio for me. The chimney goes up there and warms one corner and there's clear north light coming through a high window. I've never had it so good."

Vonnie was pleased that her mother had found a place to paint. Painting was her mother's big thing and when she was contented with her art space, she was more contented about everything else. Her mother wasn't an outgoing person and Vonnie knew their frequent moves were hard for her to adjust to, but she enjoyed her easel and her paints and she seldom complained.

"I hear there's a painting group in town that meets at the library," her mother said. "I'll check into it once we're settled. And I'm dying to visit the Nelson Gallery in the city. Imagine having a renowned gallery right at your fingertips."

"I'm glad everyone's so enthusiastic about this move," Mr. Morrison said. "Even Vonnie's off on the right foot. She met a good-looking boy this afternoon at the hardware store."

"What's his name?" her mother asked.

"Gee, Mom, I don't know. I mean, I sort of forgot to ask and he didn't say." How could she have been so dumb! And why were her folks making such a big thing over a name?

"She'll see him again at school," her father said. "You'll have time to go with her to enroll, won't you, Janice?"

Vonnie felt a sinking sensation deep inside her. "Dad! Please! I don't need anyone to go with me. All I have to do is to show up at the office. They've had new students before. And you know my records have already been forwarded here. They'll be expecting me."

"I'd better go with you, Vonnie," Mother said. "I'll want to talk to your teachers about . . . about your diabetes."

"No." The word popped out with a loud hostile sound Vonnie hadn't intended and she cleared her throat, trying to get her point across in a quieter manner. "I mean I don't want *anyone* in Roe Village to know I'm diabetic. It's really nobody's business but mine—ours. And I'm *not* a little kid anymore. I can handle any situation that comes up without any help."

"Vonnie . . ." Her mother hesitated.

"Really, Mom. I don't want *any* of the kids or teachers to know. Try to *understand*. I'm tired of being the oddball in every class, the girl who's *different*. I'm not all *that* different. We've got the disease under control. I take my shots. I watch my diet. I carry mints to take in an emergency. *What's* to go wrong?"

"Where's your bracelet, Vonnie?" Her father kept his voice carefully controlled as he looked at her bare arm, noticing the missing bracelet for the first time.

"I had it made into a necklace, Dad. I'm wearing it." She pulled it out to show both her parents. "I'm just keeping it hidden."

"Vonnie, what's come over you?" her mother asked. "You've always accepted . . . everything so gracefully, and now . . ."

Vonnie felt tears threatening to come and her throat felt tight and stiff as a lead pipe. "I'm trying to tell you, Mom. I think that this diabetes is my personal, very private problem and I resent everyone in school having to know about it."

"But your teachers need to know for your own safety," her father said. "In case there's an emergency they'll know immediately what the problem is and they can get help for you quickly."

"There won't be any emergencies," Vonnie said. "I'll see to it that there aren't."

"You can't always control emergencies," her mother said. "Sometimes too much excitement or being over-tired can trigger an insulin reaction."

"It's just not safe to keep your condition a secret," her father said.

"Dad, please." Vonnie looked her father in the eye. "Can't you guess why I was so willing to move this time?"

"I know that moving is always hard for you, for everyone, Vonnie, but . . ."

"But this time did I fuss?"

"No, no, you didn't," her father admitted, as if considering the fact for the first time.

"I was really glad to leave Washington, Dad. Really happy to leave."

"I didn't know you were that unhappy there," her mother said. "Your grades were good and you really seemed to . . ."

Grades! Couldn't her folks understand that grades weren't everything! Vonnie chose her words carefully, not wanting to be too dramatic, not wanting to seem too complaining, yet wanting to get her point across clearly once and for all.

"We only lived in Washington five months, so it wasn't all that bad. But I didn't have any dates. Not any at all."

"Some girls begin dating later than other girls," her mother said. "You mustn't let that worry you. You're a pretty girl, Vonnie. Really pretty. And when you're ready to begin dating you'll find plenty of interested boys. There's no use forcing yourself into things."

She knew her mother was trying to spare her feelings. She knew she was just average looking and she knew her mother was trying to cover up her lack of dating as a thing of her choosing, when it wasn't that way at all. "I'm ready to begin dating, Mom. I've been ready ever since the first of this year, maybe ever since the end of last year. But nobody wants to go out with a girl who has to wear a medical bracelet. Nobody wants to date a girl who they think may go into insulin shock at any minute. Normal kids just don't understand about diabetes. It scares them off."

"Now, Vonnie. You're just exaggerating," her father said.

"No, I'm not. I'm really not. Even the girls shy away from a girl with . . . problems. But this time it's going to be different. I'm going to seem just like everybody else because I'm not going to tell anyone about my shots, my diet, my . . ."

"Maybe we can reach a compromise," her father said.

"What sort of a compromise?" Vonnie asked, on guard, but willing to listen.

"Maybe we could inform the school nurse and your teachers and swear them to secrecy. Would that help?"

Vonnie hesitated, thinking carefully. A compromise might be the best arrangement she could hope for. "That might help, Dad. It might, if the teachers and nurse really kept the information top secret. But I don't want any of the kids to know. Not even one."

"Vonnie?"

Her mother spoke in such a serious tone that Vonnie looked at her with apprehension. "What, Mom?"

"I think you're blaming too much on the diabetes. I think you're expecting too much of . . . secrecy. I don't want to see you hurt and disappointed."

"What do you mean?" Vonnie asked, but deep down she guessed what her mother was about to say. And it scared her to think about it too deeply.

"You're not really an outgoing person, Vonnie. Now don't misunderstand me. There's nothing wrong with you just the way you are. But I know you're shy because I'm the same way. Some people have a hard time reaching out to others and they sometimes place the blame for this where it doesn't belong. I could join the PTA or the League of Women Voters, but I tell myself that I *have* to paint, that a club would eat up too much of my time."

"But it would, Mom. It really would."

"Not really, Vonnie. Not just one club. But deep down I know I'm just using painting as an excuse for not being outgoing. But at least I know I'm doing it, that I'm using painting as a crutch."

"You've sold a lot of your work, Mom, and you've been invited to lots of shows. You do need your free time."

"I think your mother's right, Vonnie," her father said. "I'm afraid you're going to try to hide your diabetes only to find out that it wasn't your main problem at all."

"Then let me find that out for myself, okay?" She felt vulnerable. Sometimes she thought her parents didn't understand her at all, then all at once it seemed they could see right into her very soul. It was scary. "Let me enter school as a normal girl and see what happens."

"That would be taking too much of a chance with your health, with your total well being," Dad said. "We want the best for you, Vonnie. Don't ask the impossible."

Vonnie toyed with a piece of meat ball on her plate, wishing she couldn't see her parents' point of view. But she could. She wasn't being fair to them and she knew it. They felt responsible for her and she knew she shouldn't make that responsibility harder for them.

"All right. Let's compromise. We'll tell the school nurse and my personal teachers and we'll swear them to secrecy. I'll wear the medical ID around my neck, *under* my shirt and I'll say nothing to any of the kids about any health problems I have."

"I think that's fair enough for starters," her mother said. "Maybe after you get acquainted with some friends you'll feel secure enough to . . ."

"No way, Mom. If I'm ever lucky enough to make any close friends, I'll keep them by just letting them think I'm just like they are. Deal?"

Her mother sighed. "Deal."

After they finished eating Vonnie washed the dishes, helped her mother unpack the good china, then went back to her room to finish unpacking books and pictures. In a way she felt elated. She had won part of her battle. The teachers who knew of her problem wouldn't have any influence over her popularity with the kids. And it was comforting to know that someone would know how to help her in an emergency.

3

Time seemed to race between Saturday evening and Monday morning. Vonnie completed all her unpacking, but she was still a long ways from feeling at home in her new room. Maybe she was just on edge about facing that first day at school. She practiced in her mind how she would act, from the first scene in the principal's office to the various classroom scenes. Sometimes imagining a thing before it happened made the actual happening easier. She would smile, smile, smile at everyone, but she would be wary of girls who were too eager to be too friendly too soon. Past experience had taught her that some girls would always be outsiders although they had lived in a town and attended the same school for years. She didn't intend to be snobbish, but neither did she intend to hurt feelings by rushing into quick friendships that she might soon regret.

Would she see *him?* She tried to imagine what his name might be. Hank. Or Ken. Or Mark. But there was no time to moon over his name now. How he would laugh at her if he even guessed she was interested in him after only a casual meeting over the purchase of sandpaper and steel wool!

She had laid her school clothes out the night

before after trying on at least ten outfits. First impressions were important. She had finally decided on a blue skirt and a matching turtleneck sweater that brought out the blue in her eyes. Would anyone notice? She had an earth-colored shoulder bag that matched her shoes and was large enough to carry a tiny thermos of juice and some crackers. And of course she tucked some mints into it . . . just in case. She wondered where she could go to eat her mid-morning snack without being seen. Would there be time between classes? She had to admit it was a good thing her teachers were going to know about her special problems. They would probably agree to overlook it if she were a few minutes late to her mid-morning class or if they saw her sneaking a mint during lecture or study time. If she felt faint she had to have that mint in a hurry to counteract the insulin. If things got out of balance . . . but she refused to think about that now. Once she was dressed she hurried downstairs, ate breakfast, then grabbed her coat.

"I'll drive you to school," her mother said.

"Oh, that's all right, Mom. You don't need to do that. It's just a couple of blocks. I'll walk."

"I'll drive you," her mother insisted. "I want to talk to the principal, the nurse and your teachers. Don't worry. I'll be discreet. We can probably slip inside before the bell rings and get everything taken care of ahead of class time."

Vonnie sighed. "Would you let me drive? If I have to arrive with a parent, at least let me drive. Everyone will be watching. At least we can let them know I'm sixteen and that I have my license."

"Okay, Vonnie. No reason you can't drive if you want to."

So she drove. And she parked in the lot at the side of the schoolhouse to one side of the space reserved for the school buses. The building was so old that the brick had weathered to the color of ripe plums. It was two stories tall and Vonnie could see where at least three additions had been added on to it. The bricks in the three additions were not quite matched, but the gray roof served as a common denominator unifying the whole structure.

As they walked to the big double doors with their brass handles Vonnie could feel all eyes upon her. She could almost hear the questions being whispered behind her back: Who's she? Why's she going in early? Although she wanted to shrink closer to her mother, she held her head high and kept at least a foot of space between them. Once they were inside the building she relaxed a bit. All schoolhouses smelled the same. Sweeping compound. Chalk dust. Gym lockers. She inhaled deeply of that sameness, hoping it would steady her and give her confidence. The principal's office was straight ahead of them. They stepped inside and introduced themselves to a slim blond-haired lady wearing a gray tailored suit.

"I'm Miss Chard, the principal," she said. "We're glad to have you as a new student, Veronica." She reached for a file folder on her desk. "I have your records right here."

Vonnie nodded and kept smiling as Miss Chard spoke to a pretty girl who was sharpening pencils behind the counter that separated the secretaries' desks from the waiting area.

"Allison, this is Veronica Morrison, and here is her class schedule. Will you show her where her classrooms are?"

"Yes, Miss Chard."

"Veronica, this is Allison Moore."

Vonnie nodded as she studied Allison, trying not to appear to be staring. She guessed that Allison was her own age and felt a twinge of envy at her generously curved figure. Why was her own figure so boyish! But no. She would make no comparisons, especially no comparisons that put herself down. Allison had blond hair that hung in a thick fall halfway to her waist and she wore green shoes, the brightest green shoes that Vonnie had ever seen. It was only after she had noted the hair and the shoes that she noticed that Allison was wearing gray slacks and a creamy cashmere sweater that emphasized her delicate complexion and her big brown eyes.

"Your first class will be right on this floor and right down this hall, Veronica."

"Call me Vonnie, okay? Nobody calls me Veronica but my birth certificate."

"Okay, Vonnie." Allison paused at an open doorway. "Here's your English classroom. Room A-1. Then you turn left at this corner and the third doorway on your left will be the history room. The second door is the restroom."

Their shoes grated against the concrete floor and Vonnie eyed the gray lockers that lined either side of the hallway. She wondered where her locker would be. Maybe Miss Chard would assign it later.

On the way to the history room they passed a bulletin board filled with pictures and Vonnie slowed down to look at them. Right in the center of the display was a picture of Allison in a cheerleader's outfit. Gold sweater. Green miniskirt. Under the picture was the caption: Allison Moore, Head Cheerleader. Around her picture were smaller pictures of the other cheerleaders and around those pictures were individual pictures of the members of the basketball team.

"You like basketball?" Allison asked.

"Yes. It's my favorite sport, spectator sport, that is."

"Good. We have a great team this year."

Allison seemed nice and friendly and Vonnie wondered if they would become good friends as the school year progressed. But she knew she didn't dare count on such a thing. Not at all. Cheerleaders usually had their own crowd of friends and usually it was a closed group.

"We'll have to go upstairs to your math class," Allison said. "And the Spanish room is upstairs too."

Before they reached the top of the stairs the bell rang and students flocked in from the schoolgrounds. Locker doors banged. Friends shouted to friends. And the hallway floors echoed with the footsteps of hundreds of students. Vonnie wondered if her mother had left the building yet. She hoped so. Allison was walking more quickly now and Vonnie hurried to keep up, peering quickly into the math room and then into the Spanish room. She would have no trouble finding her classes if she kept her head on straight.

They were going back downstairs when Vonnie saw *him*. Today he was wearing jeans and a yellow V-neck pullover over a white cotton shirt. He smiled and spoke to her, then walked on down the hallway. Vonnie could feel her heart pounding and her hands felt damply warm. Could Allison hear her heart?

"You know Pete?" Allison asked, surprise coloring her tone.

Pete. His name was Pete. It suited him. Vonnie blinked and she could still see the after image of his dark hair and blue eyes on the inside of her eyelids.

"No, I don't know him. Not really. I just accidentally met him Saturday at the hardware store while I was doing errands for my folks."

"Pete Karmer," Allison said, giving Vonnie a sidelong glance. "He usually keeps pretty much to himself since . . ."

"Since what?" Vonnie blurted the question, her curiosity more than she could curtail.

"Since Gabrielle . . . died."

"His sister?"

Again Allison gave her a sidelong glance. "His girlfriend. He doesn't have any sisters."

"What happened to Gabrielle? It sounds really sad."

"Of course it was sad," Allison agreed. "Everyone liked Gabrielle and everyone likes Pete. We've all known both of them since we were in grade school. Gabrielle died suddenly—pneumonia. We could hardly believe it."

Questions churned in Vonnie's mind yet she didn't dare ask them. Was Pete still grieving? Had he and Gabrielle been steadies? Or maybe they had been engaged. "Poor Pete," she said lamely.

"Pete hasn't been the same since," Allison said. "Everyone's been really nice to him and all the girls flirt with him like mad, but he doesn't pay any attention. It's as if he's closed himself in a shell and nobody can reach him." Then Allison's voice took on a happier tone. "Here we are back at square one. If you hurry you can make it into your English class before the late bell rings."

"Thank you for showing me around," Vonnie said. "I really appreciate it."

"You're welcome, Vonnie. See you around."

And she was gone. Vonnie went into English class, introduced herself to the teacher and received her seat assignment along with a quick introduction to the class. She smiled. And she kept smiling. But she hardly realized what was going on around her. She wanted to know more about Pete Karmer, more about Gabrielle. What was her last name? How serious had Pete been over her? Vonnie felt a mixture of emotions. She felt a sadness for an unknown girl who had died so young. And she was sympathetic toward Pete Karmer who had lost a special friend. Yet Allison's words had had a superficial quality about them, a detached quality that made Vonnie wonder if she had been telling the whole truth of the matter. "It's as if he's closed himself in a shell and nobody can reach him," Allison had said, yet Vonnie had felt no difficulty in reaching Pete when she was in the hardware store on Saturday. He had seemed friendly and outgoing. Far more friendly and outgoing than she had been in return. Maybe Allison Moore was subtly telling her that Pete Karmer was off limits. Maybe Allison had her eye on him.

But no. Vonnie guessed that Allison Moore could have any guy in school as her boyfriend by merely smiling at him. She was beautiful. She was head cheerleader. No doubt Allison was queen of the school's "in" group. She had probably been telling the truth about Pete. Pete's friendliness at the store had probably been an act he forced himself to perform to keep his job. Shopkeepers wouldn't tolerate a grumpy sales clerk. Surely Pete had been smiling through tears she hadn't been perceptive enough to see. But he had remembered her. He had spoken to her again today. And he had smiled. She wondered if he knew her name.

She sat through English class and history class, then it was time for her snack. She wasn't hungry, but her doctor insisted on small between-meal snacks to keep her body chemistry in balance. The moment of truth, she thought. Where could she go and be unnoticed? She didn't want any kids to be whispering about the freaky girl sneaking orange juice at ten o'clock.

The nurse's office? Maybe she could go there. But where was it? She didn't know. She headed down the hall, then went into the girls' restroom. Three girls were leaving and she was in luck. An alcove just off the restroom held a canvas cot. A green curtain suspended from the ceiling hung around the cot. Quickly Vonnie slipped into the alcove and pulled the curtain for privacy. Once she felt secure she unzipped her shoulder bag, removed her thermos and poured juice into the thermos cap. She ate her crackers, washing them down with the juice, then hid the thermos inside her bag, stepped from the curtained cubicle and hurried to the media center to spend her free period.

Nobody questioned her. She was home free as far as her first snacktime was concerned. At noon she ate soup and fruit with her mother in their big old kitchen, then she returned to school for the afternoon.

Math class required her full attention and she was glad Spanish was last because she liked it and because she liked her partner, Hannah Gordon, with her persimmon-colored hair and her branflake sprinkling of freckles on nose and cheekbones. Hannah had a plump-pillow figure, a bouncy walk, but it was her friendly smile that made Vonnie feel less like a newcomer.

"You're stuck with me, Vonnie," Hannah said. "I'm really no good at Spanish, but maybe we can help each other read and translate."

And that's the way it worked out. Vonnie knew she was good at Spanish and it made her feel needed to be able to help Hannah.

"Where to you live?" Hannah asked as they headed for their lockers when the final bell rang.

"The old Williams place. Know where it is?"

"Sure. I live just three blocks beyond it. We can walk home together . . . that is, if you're going home right now."

Vonnie was torn between accepting Hannah's invitation and in spending a little more time in the media center. She had wanted to look up last year's school yearbook. You could find out a lot about kids by reading a yearbook and she wanted to know more about Pete Karmer and most of all about Gabrielle. But she put her curiosity aside and smiled at Hannah.

"Sure, I'm going right home. Be glad to have some company."

"It's sort of lonesome when you're new in a school, I imagine," Hannah said.

"Right. It can be. But everyone here seems friendly." Vonnie said the words although she wasn't sure she meant them. What everyone had really seemed was . . . disinterested. Oh, sure, Pete had spoken to her, but anyone would have done the same. And Allison had shown her around the school, but it was her job as early-morning student assistant. Of course, Hannah seemed friendly enough, but then, they were living in the same area and it was no big deal to walk home together.

Still it had been a good day. She had kept her secret. She had survived. She and Hannah walked along without speaking for a while, then Vonnie spoke up.

"Did you know Gabrielle, Hannah? I mean Allison was telling me about her and . . . I can't seem to get the story out of my mind. It's really sad."

"Yeah. It's sad. We all knew Gabrielle. We all felt shaken about her death . . . especially Pete Karmer. Pneumonia. Sick just two days. And that was it. But how did you know about her?"

"I told you. Allison mentioned her to me when she was showing me to my classrooms this morning."

"Yeah. Allison's always liked Pete. Or maybe I should say that Pete has always offered Allison a challenge. She always wants the boy she can't get."

"You don't sound as if you like her very much."

"Oh, she's okay. She's really popular around school. It's just that Allison's always after what's good for Allison. And I think she's show-offy with those green shoes. Gold and green are school colors, so since her hair's gold she always wears green shoes so she'll always show the school colors. Sometimes Allison can be a bit much."

"Well, at least she has school spirit." Vonnie chose her words carefully, determined not to say anything she might regret later. When they came to her house, she considered inviting Hannah in, then thought better of it. Best not to seem too eager at first. She was the new girl in school and she knew she was up for observation.

"See you tomorrow, Hannah."

"*Hasta la vista,*" Hannah said, smiling. "I think you're going to be the best thing that's happened to my Spanish grade in ages, Vonnie. See ya."

4

Home. Vonnie said the word to herself as she looked at the old Victorian house sitting like a dignified turn-of-the-century lady all decked out in curlicues and furbelows. Home. This was home from now on—for a while at least. She turned the brass knob, opened the door and stepped inside, watching the way the primary colors of the fanlight played across the oak floor. She petted Loboy who ran to greet her and relaxed. She had survived her first day at Roe Village High. Tomorrow she wouldn't feel quite so "new" and the school wouldn't seem quite so different.

"That you, Vonnie?" her mother's voice called from a great distance and Vonnie guessed she was up on the third floor trying to organize her art studio.

"It's me," Vonnie called back, glad someone was there. "Home and hungry." She could smell the faint odor of turpentine as her mother appeared at the head of the stairway wearing jeans and painter's smock, her pixie-style hair tousled. Good, Vonnie thought. When she's painting she's happy. Sometimes her mother's moods were like hair spray. They misted over everyone nearby. She wondered if it worked the other way too. Maybe when *she* was happy the whole family benefited. She smiled and it wasn't a forced smile. The first day of school had gone as well as could be expected.

"I'll have a snack with you," her mother said. "I'm dying to hear all about your day."

"Okay, Mom." Vonnie hung up her jacket and got ready for the after-school ritual. She was supposed to have a snack each day a couple of hours before dinner and her mother usually joined her. It gave them a chance to talk and Vonnie looked on it as a special time in her day. Sharing snacks with someone who understood made her diabetes a lot easier to bear.

She washed her hands, then went to the refrigerator for cheese and milk. Her mother set glasses and a plate of saltines on the table and they both sat down.

"How did it go?" her mother asked, pouring milk into the glasses.

"Fine. I like all the teachers and I'm ahead of the class in Spanish. I was afraid I'd be behind and have to cram to catch up on vocabulary and verb forms."

"Did you have art?"

"No. That's a Tuesday–Thursday class. I'll meet that teacher tomorrow."

"Did you meet any nice kids?"

Vonnie tasted the sharpness of the cheese and washed it down with some milk. "I met Allison Moore, the girl who showed me around, the one you saw early this morning. And there's a neat girl in my Spanish class. Hannah Gordon. She lives near here too. We walked home together."

"You could have invited her in."

"I suppose so. But I didn't want to push, to seem too eager. You know how it is. How was your day? You've been painting?"

"Yes. I've arranged my easel and paints in the attic by the north window. I'm going to have a great studio up there—lots of room and no reason to worry about the mess. I've never had it so good."

Vonnie respected her mother's artistic talent and wished she would hang more of her paintings in their home, but she never did. She usually hung one painting at a time in a special spot, then changed the paintings frequently on the theory that after a week nobody really noticed the spot unless there was something new to look at. She had a point. Vonnie always noticed the changing of the paintings.

"What are you working on, Mom?"

"A still life. But as soon as the weather warms up a bit more I'm going to do landscapes. I hear there's a creek, some stone bridges and lots of interesting fountains in the Plaza district of the city."

"Sounds great. I'd like to go with you sometime if you ever go on a Saturday or Sunday. I might try some sketches too."

"It's a deal, Vonnie. And I think springtime comes early around here. I hope so, anyway."

"Mom, about the diabetes. How many people did you tell?" She held her breath, waiting for her mother's reply.

"I told the principal—in her office. Nobody else heard and she promised to keep the matter private. Then I visited with each of your classroom teachers and the school nurse. They all understood your position, Vonnie. Your secret is safe and I'll feel easier knowing that people who can help you are aware of the situation."

Vonnie sighed. It was the best she could hope for under the circumstances. "Thanks, Mom. I found a private place to eat my snack. I think everything is going to work out okay."

When they had finished eating Vonnie cleared the table, then went upstairs to her room. She only had a smidgen of homework—one chapter of reading for history class, three pages of Spanish translation. She finished in an hour. She sort of hoped Hannah would call her for help with the Spanish, but the phone didn't ring. She tried not to feel disappointed. She had no idea of Hannah's schedule. Maybe she did her studying after dinner instead of after school.

She closed her books and walked to her closet. What would she wear tomorrow? The first days in a new school were always so important, the days when everybody was looking her over, sizing her up. She took off her blue skirt and turtleneck and put on jeans and a gingham shirt, then studied her wardrobe.

The girl with the shy-blue eyes. That's what Dad called her when he wanted to tease a bit about her shyness. And she didn't mind. She guessed her eyes were her best asset. But she had played up the blue eyes today. Now what about tomorrow? Lots of girls had been wearing slacks. She pulled out the tan twills with Levi on the pocket. She would wear them with the burnished bronze shirt that almost matched her hair. She hung the two garments together on the center of the clothes rod then went to her jewelry box. A gold chain. No, two gold chains—one long and one short. And a gold bracelet. No, cancel the bracelet. That was too much. She didn't want to overdo anything. Better go with too little than too much.

She picked up a Phyllis Whitney suspense novel and had just settled down to read when she heard her father's car in the driveway. She gave her parents a few minutes together, then ran downstairs. Ever since she was a little kid her dad's arrival had been an important moment in her day.

"Hi, Dad. How did it go in the big city?" She moved in close for the hug he always offered. She liked the smell of lemon drops on his breath, liked it much better than the cigarette odor that had clung to him and his clothes before he gave up smoking.

"Everything went fine, Vonnie. Just fine. I'll be working with a lot of nice, efficient people."

"If they're so nice and efficient why were you called in?" She smiled to herself. Dad always looked on the bright side of things. Maybe that's what made him so good at his job.

"Even efficient people sometimes have production problems, Vonnie. But how was your day?"

"Fine. The teachers are neat and I'm not behind in any classes."

"And the kids?"

"They're going to be fine too, Dad. I can't get acquainted with everyone the first day, you know."

"Of course not." Her father poured himself a big glass of iced tea and carried it upstairs with him as he went to change into slacks and a sweater.

"Can I help with dinner, Mom?"

"You can set the table. And you can make us individual salads if you want to. Lettuce and carrot and celery. Just use the small wooden bowls. And we'll all use your special dressing tonight. Your dad likes it better than what I buy at the store."

She began her chores, appreciating the way her parents tried to make her diet seem pleasant. And really it wasn't so bad. She could eat a variety of things. It was just a matter of planning and that was fairly easy as long as she was eating at home. It was the eating-out situations with kids that posed a problem. Everyone always ordered burgers and fries and candy bars. It was the pits always having to order a diet cola and to pretend she wasn't hungry or that she was trying to lose a few pounds.

Her mother had prepared pot roast for their dinner, which Vonnie always liked, especially the onions and carrots. Tonight she would skip the potato.

"Got lots of homework?" her father asked when they were seated at the table.

"A little." She didn't tell him she had already done it. "I'd like to go to the library and get some books we're going to need for English class." That was the truth. The teacher had mentioned a research paper that would be due soon, but she really wanted to go to the library to look at the school yearbooks. Gabrielle. She had to know more about Gabrielle. . . . She didn't even know her last name. But surely there wouldn't be more than one girl in the sophomore class named Gabrielle.

"The library," her father mused. "Do you know where it is?"

"No. But in a town the size of Roe Village it shouldn't be too hard to find. I'll look up the address in the phone book."

"Maybe I'll go with you to the library," her mother said. "I'd like to see what art books they have in the stacks."

Vonnie's heart sank. She had wanted to go alone.

"Well, if you're both going out maybe I can get you to run an errand for me," Mr. Morrison said.

"Sure, Dad. What is it?" She sipped her milk, then looked at her father.

"I need some more things from the hardware store. Some paint thinner. Some putty. And some of those putty sticks that you use to fill nail holes."

She felt her heart beating a little faster than usual. Would Pete Karmer be working tonight? "Make me a list, okay?"

"But is the hardware store open on Monday night?" her mother asked.

"Roe Village stores stay open on Monday nights until eight-thirty," Mr. Morrison said. "I noticed the sign in the hardware store window when we were there Saturday."

There was no dishwasher in the house so after they finished eating Vonnie washed the dinner dishes and stacked them in the drainer to dry. She looked at her clothes. Yes. She could go to the library in jeans. Probably all the kids did. She wished her mother weren't going along. Would she wonder why Vonnie was interested in last year's yearbook? Maybe she wouldn't. There was certainly nothing wrong with being interested in the kids you were going to school with.

She went upstairs, combed her hair carefully and applied a touch of eye shadow and mascara that made her eyes seem bigger and bluer. And she grabbed her blue jacket.

"Ready, Mom?" she asked as she reached the foot of the stairs and paused at the living room doorway.

"Do you mind going alone, Vonnie? I've got caught up in this TV program and suddenly just relaxing here at home seems very appealing."

"It's okay, Mom." She tried to keep relief from sounding in her voice. "I won't get lost. Can I bring you anything from the library?"

"No. I'll go take a look another day. Thanks."

43

"Here's the list for the hardware store." Her father jotted one more item in his bold script before he folded the slip of paper and gave it to her. "And tell that good-looking fellow in there hello for me."

She felt herself blushing. Did Dad really need this stuff from the store, or was he just trying to play matchmaker?

"Here's a signed check, Vonnie." He ripped the check from the checkbook and handed it to her. "You can fill in the correct amount at the store. And here are the car keys. Drive carefully."

She took the check and the keys, pleased that her folks trusted her with the car. "I'll be home around nine or before," she said.

She backed the red Chevette carefully from the driveway and headed for town. She could smell the soft dampness of spring in the cool night air and the sky was like a black velvet cap sequined with stars. She heard the clear low call of a bird she couldn't recognize. A low trill. A plaintive cry. Then a high warble. She would have to ask someone what it was.

As she reached the brightly lighted town square her hands began to perspire. Would Pete be working? Would he think she was deliberately seeking him out? She hoped not. She was glad the list was in her dad's handwriting. She would just give it to him and let him fill it for her. Then when he saw her dad's signature on the check he'd know she hadn't come here on some whim of her own.

She had to drive around the courtyard square twice before she found a parking place. Then she had to walk over a block to the hardware store. Many shoppers were hurrying along the sidewalk. Car horns honked. Friends called to one another.

Music blared from a combination pool hall and lounge. Clearly Monday night was a big night in Roe Village. She hurried on toward Johnson's Hardware, then slowed down just before she reached the door, not wanting to seem in a hurry.

Tonight the store smelled of paint thinner and cigar smoke and stale grease from the diner next door, but she hardly noticed as she looked for Pete, all the time trying not to appear to be looking for anyone special. He wasn't in sight. Maybe he was in the stock room. Or maybe he was on dinner break. Or maybe . . .

"May I help you, Miss?" A baldheaded man approached her, smiling.

Vonnie's mouth was so dry she had to swallow before she could answer. "Yes, thank you. My father wants a few things." And she read off the list. In a matter of five minutes the clerk had placed the items in a sack and was making change for her. No Pete. But why was she so disappointed?

There was no denying the feeling. She had hoped to see him. She had wanted to see him. And she was disappointed that he wasn't there. She had never seen a boy who had seemed so special to her on such short acquaintance. She wondered if Pete had thought there was anything special about her. Probably not. She wasn't the kind of girl who stood out in a crowd.

She put the sack of supplies in the trunk of the car, drove on to the library, then parked and went inside. She liked libraries. There was a friendliness about them that seemed to welcome everyone. And the Roe Village library was no exception. The square building was gray limestone on the outside, but inside it was warm and alive with color. Bright

blue carpeting covered the floor and vinyl uphol-
stered easy chairs in jewel tones of gold, pink and
pale green dotted the reading room. French im-
pressionistic prints hung on the buff-colored
walls, brightly colored prints that could be checked
out like books and kept for three weeks. The room
was cushioned in a comfortable silence, broken
only by the distant rhythmic whir of a copy ma-
chine.

"May I help you?" a green-smocked lady with hair
the fragile texture of spun glass asked Vonnie from
her position behind a central desk.

"I'd like to apply for a library card," Vonnie said.
She gave the necessary information, paid the twenty-
five cent handling fee and received a temporary
card.

"Is there something special I can help you find?"
the lady asked.

"I'd like to see the local high school yearbooks,
please."

"They're in our reference room," the lady replied.
"We don't check them out to patrons, but you're
welcome to look at them there."

"Thank you." She hurried to the reference room
which looked much the same as the reading room.
She found the thin green and gold volumes quickly,
pulled out last year's edition and turned the slick
pages until she came to the section on the sophomore class.

She saw Pete's picture first. It fairly leaped off the
page at her. Even in the formal picture he hadn't
been able to make the cowlick on his crown lie flat.
He looked very solemn in dark suit, white shirt and
tie, and his eyes seemed to look at the world with
calm understanding. She studied the picture for

several moments before she continued scanning the page.

There. She saw the name. Gabrielle. Gabrielle Channing. And she was beautiful. Vonnie had known Gabrielle would be beautiful. Dark hair framed her oval face and hung with a slight curl to her shoulders. A heavy fringe of sooty lashes accented her wide-spaced dark eyes and, although she wasn't smiling in the picture, her mouth turned up slightly at the corners as if she were always about to smile.

Suddenly Vonnie felt as if she were prying into Pete's private life, into his private sorrow. She snapped the yearbook shut quickly and replaced it on the shelf, wishing she hadn't come here. She had liked Pete Karmer's looks, his friendliness and she had wanted to know him better. But now a sense of hopelessness washed over her. What was the use! She couldn't compete with a ghost—a beautiful ghost.

5

On Tuesday morning Vonnie stayed in her room until she heard her parents go downstairs. Then she rose and shampooed her hair. Sometimes she got tired of hearing her mother's prediction that she would be bald before she was thirty if she shampooed every day. And she thought her father's jokes about buying stock in the shampoo company were growing thin.

She wanted to look her best, especially this first week of school and she couldn't look her best unless her hair was fluffy, unless it had that shiny, just-washed look. She wondered if Pete would notice her today. But why should he? He hadn't even seen her in class yesterday. It seemed almost impossible that two juniors wouldn't have at least one class together.

After she dried her Dutch bob with the blow comb she dressed carefully in the earth-colored slacks outfit she had decided upon the day before, slipped the gold chains around her neck and hurried downstairs to breakfast. Her parents were already eating, her mother in jeans and a navy sweatshirt, her dad in his dark business suit. She made herself a soft-boiled egg to go along with her juice and cereal before she joined them.

"Anything special going on at school this week?" her father asked.

"Just a basketball game on Friday night, Dad. At least that's the only thing I know about."

"Are you going to go to it?" her mother asked.

"I don't know." She didn't want to go to the game alone, but she didn't say so. She didn't want her parents feeling concerned about her social life. "It's sort of hard to get excited about a ball team when they only have a game or two left in the season."

"Did you find the books you needed at the library?" her mother asked. "I didn't notice you bringing anything home."

"I'll have to go back again, Mom. I started looking at old high school yearbooks and the time just slipped away. I wanted to find out what activities the school offers and who participates. You can learn a lot about a school by reading the yearbook."

"I'd guess he was a basketball player," her father said with a twinkle in his eye.

"Who?" Vonnie asked, feeling her neck begin to grow warm.

"The boy in the hardware store. What's his name?"

"His name's Pete Karmer."

"Then you've met him again?"

She hated it when Dad pried in his half-teasing, half-serious way. "He wasn't at the hardware store last night, if that's what you mean, but I did see him at school. We don't have any classes together though."

"Too bad." Her dad shrugged. "But I'm sure there are other boys around. You look nice in that outfit, Vonnie."

"Thanks, Dad."

She ate her breakfast quickly, almost relieved when her father left for his short drive into the city. She gave herself her insulin shot, then gathered her books. She hoped she might meet Hannah on the way to school. It would be nice to arrive with someone this morning. She slipped into her jacket.

"Have a good day, Vonnie," her mother said.

"You too, Mom. I'll see you at noon." She gave Loboy a pat before she stepped onto the porch and closed the door behind herself.

The sun was slanting golden rays through the bare maple branches but the air felt crisp. Wisps of smoke hung like white plumes above the red brick chimneys across the street, but she inhaled the damp earth-smell that promised spring. Spring! She could hardly wait.

She looked down the street toward Hannah's house, but she saw nobody on the sidewalk. Maybe Hannah rode to school with someone. Or maybe she had gone early for a special meeting. Or . . . No use speculating on Hannah's activities. The bottom line was that she was going to have to arrive at school alone. And then what? She could hardly barge up to a group and start talking. Nor could she just stand around alone.

She walked very slowly, hoping she wouldn't arrive too soon before the bell rang. When she reached the schoolyard Hannah stepped from a group of girls and bounced toward her. Today Hannah was wearing a lime green jumpsuit and her orangy hair glinted in the sunlight.

"Hi, Vonnie. Got a message for you."

"What sort of a message?" She smiled in friendliness and in relief at not being quite so alone. Hannah seemed to have a whole group of friends.

Vonnie hoped she would introduce her to some of them. But she didn't.

"Miss Chard asked me to watch for you. She wants to see you in her office." Then when Hannah saw the worried expression on Vonnie's face she continued, "Hey, no sweat. It's just something about your locker."

"Thanks, Hannah. I'd better go see about it." She smiled at Hannah again, then hurried inside. Empty schoolhouses were like empty shells, strangely hollow and "echoey." And all the smells seemed magnified. Today the fragrance of sage drifted up from the cafeteria.

She had wondered about a locker yesterday, but she had been too busy to ask and then when she had had a chance to walk with Hannah after school she had forgotten all about lockers.

Today Miss Chard was wearing a navy blue suit that made a nice contrast to her blond hair and she smiled as Vonnie entered the office.

"Good morning, Vonnie." She pushed a combination lock toward her across the counter. "Sorry we didn't get a locker assigned to you yesterday. Here's a lock and you can use locker 231. It's right down the central hallway to your right."

"Thank you, Miss Chard. I needed to take my new textbooks home with me yesterday to review, but I'm glad to have the locker today."

"You may put your things into it now before the bell rings, if you care to. And practice with the lock a couple of times until you have the combination memorized."

"I will. Thank you." She took the lock and left the office. Moments later she found her locker, hung her jacket inside and laid her books on the upper shelf

51

while she worked with the combination. Ten to the right. Forty-nine to the left. Thirty-five to the right. And it opened. She locked it and worked the combination again to be sure. The bell rang just as she finished and she watched students pour into the hallway, their feet sounding more like a herd of cattle than a group of people, as shoes pounded and scraped against the concrete floor.

A math book flew through the air and was caught a second before it crashed into a trophy case. Music from a transistor blared, then stopped abruptly. Vonnie lifted her English and history texts from the shelf where she had laid them and when she turned she saw Allison Moore at the locker next to hers. Allison was wearing a green sweater that brought out the green in her eyes and matched her shoes and her long blond hair hung forward, framing her face. All at once Vonnie felt like a nerd in the dull-colored outfit she had chosen. How could clothes that seemed subtly charming at home seem so frumpy now!

Allison was smiling brightly and Vonnie smiled back, ready to speak until suddenly she realized that Allison's smile was for someone just behind her. Her lips felt like rubber bands stretched to the breaking point and she turned her head slightly and pretended to hunt a pencil in her locker.

"Hi, Chad," Allison said to a tall red-haired boy. "Did you finish that math assignment?"

"Sure," Chad answered. "No big deal."

"I thought it was a big deal." Allison looked up at Chad through a fringe of dark lashes. "Old Alexander will flip when he sees I didn't get it at all."

"Maybe I can help you at noon," Chad offered.

"Oh, would you, Chad?" Allison moistened her

lower lip and smiled again. "You'd really save my life if you could help me."

"See you in the lunch room," Chad said. "Got to get down to typing now."

Her boyfriend, Vonnie thought. She probably dates the whole basketball team. Everyone will have a boyfriend except me. And girlfriends too. She closed her locker door and snapped the lock and when she looked up again Allison was looking directly at her. She was sure this time. Had Allison been watching her? Vonnie felt uneasy, but she smiled again and spoke.

"Hi, Allison." Why couldn't she think of something else to say?

"Oh, hi, Lonnie. Nice to see you."

"Vonnie. My name's *Vonnie."* She felt herself flush. There was something about saying her own name that always made her self-conscious.

"Oh sure!" Allison smiled again. "Sorry. I knew it was a diminutive of some sort. Just got the first letter mixed up."

A diminutive. Is that how Allison thought of her? Something small and unimportant? Before Vonnie could reply another boy stopped at Allison's locker. Tall. Did she *really* date the whole ball team? This boy had long brown hair and soft cocker-spaniel eyes and he looked from Allison to Vonnie.

"Am I interrupting something, girls?"

"No way." Allison fluttered her lashes and smiled up at him much as she had smiled at Chad. Then when the boy continued to look questioningly at Vonnie, Allison stopped smiling.

"This is Vonnie Norris, Jeff. Vonnie, Jeff Jenks."

"Vonnie *Morrison."* She emphasized her last name for Allison's benefit, again feeling very self-conscious. "Nice to know you, Jeff. See you around." She smiled and hurried on toward the English room. *Lonnie Norris.* That's how much of an impression she had made on Allison Moore yesterday. She had a feeling that Allison remembered few details where girls were concerned.

Vonnie smiled at Miss Biskis standing slim and tall and ramrod straight in her black dress and shoes. Fifty. She must be at least fifty, Vonnie thought. Then as she took her seat, she opened her book and pretended to review the day's assignment. Gradually the class assembled and Vonnie looked around her. The room was filled with dark oak chairs, each with one wide arm that served as a writing area. Allison was sitting in the middle of the center row. The redhead named Chad was sitting behind her and Hannah sat next to him. Vonnie smiled at Hannah, thinking she looked a lot like Chad except for being much shorter. Had Hannah been in this class yesterday? She probably had, Vonnie thought, and she just hadn't realized it. She looked down at her book once more, not glancing up until a shadow fell across her page.

"We meet again, Vonnie."

The low resonant voice. She knew before she raised her head that it was Pete Karmer and suddenly her tongue was like a blotter against the roof of her mouth and she was afraid she couldn't speak. Today he was wearing a gray V-neck and dark brown cords that matched his hair. He smiled at her. She could smell a faint odor of leather about him. But how could she think of leather when he was smiling at her like that?

"Hi," she said, not using his name, reluctant to let him know that she knew it. Yet he had shown no reluctance at knowing her name. How had he learned it? She knew he hadn't been in class yesterday. She had looked for him. She would have remembered if he had been present. Then her sudden spurt of excitement at seeing him faded as quickly as it had erupted when he eased along the row behind her and plopped his books on the desk arm of the chair next to Allison's.

Hannah's words replayed in Vonnie's mind as she turned her head slightly so she could see Pete and Allison from the corner of her eye: Pete has always offered Allison a challenge. Maybe Pete wasn't such a challenge to Allison after all. He had chosen to sit beside her, hadn't he? Or had she chosen to sit beside him? Or maybe Miss Biskis had assigned their seating.

She saw Jeff Jenks on the other side of Allison. Clearly, Allison was Queen Bee wherever she went. Vonnie straightened in her chair and faced the front of the room as Miss Biskis began talking about the English assignment.

The class had been studying the structure of the short story and Miss Biskis devoted the whole period to analyzing a short story from the English textbook. Vonnie took notes. Everybody was taking notes. And toward the end of the hour Miss Biskis announced a new project.

"I've organized the class into teams of two," she began. "I want each team to write a brief analysis of 'The Lottery.' In your analysis you're to note where the beginning of the story ends, where the middle starts, where the ending starts. And please include an explanation of how the story climax proves a theme or a universal truth. I want each of you to discuss the story with your teammate. When two minds come together, sometimes a third mind is formed that can offer valuable insights into a problem."

Groans filled the room when Miss Biskis paused and she tapped on her desk with the edge of a ballpoint. "Listen carefully to your team assignments, please. Dick and Jim. Sue and Marty. Hannah and Pete. Allison and Chad. Vonnie and Jeff."

Vonnie stopped listening as soon as she heard her name. At least she knew who Jeff was. She wondered if he was a good English student and she realized he was probably wondering the same thing about her. When two minds come together. . . . As the dismissal bell rang Jeff overtook her before she was out the door.

"Hey, Vonnie, where can we get together to work on this assignment? How about during lunch hour?"

She felt an icy chill at the base of her spine. Trouble already. "Can't do it, Jeff. I go home for lunch."

Jeff raised an eyebrow. "Every day? I mean . . ."

"I do go home every day," she said. "Maybe we could get together in the media center after school."

"No way. I've got basketball practice. But maybe we could meet at the public library after supper."

"That might work out."

"And again it might not," Allison said, joining them. She frowned at Vonnie, then smiled up at Jeff. "You know we have plans for every night this week, Jeff."

"Well, the English assignment has to be done sometime," Jeff said. "And Vonnie . . ."

Vonnie felt Allison laying a guilt trip on her with her quick scowling glance, but when she spoke she addressed Jeff. "Surely you two can get together during some lunch hour."

"Vonnie goes home for lunch."

"So she can stay here one day," Allison said. "What's the big deal about lunch!"

"No," Vonnie said. "I really can't." She made no further explanation, but she felt shaky inside. Guilty. She had read a book on being assertive and the author had said that a person didn't owe others explanations for personal behavior. But she had trouble believing that. Assertiveness was easier to read about than it was to practice. However, necessity made her stand firm.

"So we'll trade partners," Allison said. "Jeff, you and Chad can work together and Vonnie and I will work together. Biskis won't care."

"Is that okay with you, Vonnie?" Jeff asked, clearly relieved.

"Yes. That'll be fine. And thanks, Allison. Maybe we can get together after school, okay?" She relaxed a bit. Maybe the team change was going to be fine. At least it would give her a chance to become better acquainted with Allison.

"I hope you're not going to come on like a grind, Vonnie." Allison giggled. "You write your analysis of the story and I'll write mine, then we can meet some morning before school and piece them together. No big deal."

"Fine." Vonnie felt completely deflated. Allison hadn't really wanted to work with her. She just hadn't wanted Jeff working with her . . . or Chad. Again Hannah's words echoed in her thoughts: Allison's always after what's good for Allison.

Vonnie had hoped that Pete might say something

more to her after class, but of course he hadn't had a chance to with Allison and Jeff crowding around talking about the team assignment and all. And Hannah and Pete were English partners. He had probably been talking to Hannah. Why couldn't Miss Biskis have paired her off with Pete? But miracles didn't happen nowadays. That would have been too much to hope for. She would accept Allison and make the best of it.

In history class Vonnie soon forgot the problems over the English assignment. When she left the history room she was still so caught up in the discussion of the Civil War that Pete had to touch her arm to get her attention. She all but melted right there on the floor when she saw him again.

"Going to the media center?" he asked.

She wished she could say yes, wished she could walk along with him, but she didn't dare. She could feel the hard outline of her thermos bottle pushing against the thin fabric of her shoulder bag like a silent reminder of duty.

"I'll be in the center in a few minutes, Pete, but I have an errand to take care of first."

"Oh . . . well . . . okay."

She turned and headed toward the restroom, feeling as if a vise were squeezing her heart. There was something so final about those three words Pete had spoken. Surely he had thought she was brushing him off. Why was everything working out so rotten for her today? Maybe Pete would think she had a steady boyfriend in her old hometown. Maybe he wouldn't even try to talk to her again. She had blown it! She felt tears of frustration stinging her eyelids as she opened the door to the girls' room.

6

Today groups of chattering girls had headed for the restroom like bees to the hive and in her need to be alone Vonnie stalled for time, combing her hair, washing her hands. When at last the room cleared out she stepped into the alcove and pulled the green privacy curtain. She wolfed her snack so quickly that the Wheat Thins crumbs stuck in her throat and she almost choked before she could wash them down with the tomato juice.

What was Pete thinking of her! He probably had her pegged as a class-one snob. Yet their first meeting at the hardware store should have told him she wasn't a snob. Or should it? She remembered all too clearly her shyness and her trouble in carrying on a smooth conversation with him.

The deserted restroom was like a tiled echo chamber and her footsteps reverberated hollowly as she left it and hurried to the carpeted quiet of the media center. She saw Pete sitting on a straight-backed chair at a round reading table near the windows at the back of the room. Jeff and a boy she didn't know were sitting with him. Jeff's book was on the table and he propped his jaw on his hand as he read, but Pete was leaning back in his chair resting his book on his belt buckle. She couldn't join them. No way. If Pete had been alone she might have slipped into a seat across from him, but she couldn't plunk herself down at a table already occupied by three boys. The word would flash through the school like a news brief on TV: Vonnie Morrison is a chaser.

She chose a chair carefully, one some distance from Pete and his friends, yet directly in his line of vision, should he glance up. Maybe he would join her. She laid her notebook on the table, turned to "The Lottery" in her English text and began to read. She read the whole story for an overview, then she returned to the beginning and began analyzing it. Word count. Number of characters. Plot line. She marked the place where she thought the beginning ended. Did a story beginning always take up a fifth of the total wordage? This one seemed to. She made a note of that fact.

But as she worked part of her mind was on Pete. Minutes passed and he didn't join her. Maybe he thought his friends would kid him. Or maybe he was thinking of Gabrielle. Gabrielle. She wished she hadn't looked up her picture, wished she didn't know what a doll Gabrielle had been. Whatever Pete must be thinking, she didn't want to be placed in another awkward position when the dismissal bell rang and lunch hour began.

She rose and walked toward the doorway leading into the hall, stopping near that exit and pretending interest in a display of *National Geographic*s. When the bell rang, she hurried into the hall and headed for her locker.

"Vonnie! Hey, Vonnie!"

She stopped and turned at the sound of Hannah's

throaty voice rising above a rush of chatter and laughter. There was safety in numbers and she didn't want Pete to approach her now, not now when she would have to give him another brushoff. But she needn't have worried. Pete was nowhere in sight.

"Hi, Hannah. What's up?" Vonnie paused until Hannah caught up with her, then they walked on toward her locker.

"I'd like you to meet some of my friends in the cafeteria, Vonnie." Hannah balanced her books on her right hip and eased a pen into the pocket of her green jumpsuit. "Sometimes it's hard to find a seat, but our crowd sits at a table near the north wall. I'll save you a place if you want to join us."

Again Vonnie knew she was on the spot and she felt a muscle tighten and twist in the pit of her stomach. Was she going to turn everyone off on this second day of school! She forced a bright smile. "Thanks a bunch, Hannah. I'd love to sit with you and meet your friends, but I go home at noon."

"You *do? Every* day?"

Vonnie nodded, remembering that she didn't have to explain, but biting her tongue in an effort not to do so. "Maybe I can meet your friends after school."

Hannah shook her head, sending her fiery pony tale into motion. "That's not so easy, Vonnie. Most of the kids have after-school jobs or basketball practice or something."

"Well, maybe we can get together before school sometimes. I could get here lots earlier than I did today."

"Maybe so. But lunch hour is the time the kids really get together to talk over things." A pleading tone sounded in Hannah's voice, a tone that told

Vonnie Hannah thought she might be able to wheedle her into changing her mind. She steeled herself to be firm and wished she couldn't smell an oniony fragrance wafting from the kitchen and making her mouth water.

"I really appreciate the invite, Hannah. I wish I could stay. Maybe I can get back early, before everyone takes off for afternoon classes."

Hannah brightened, nodded. "Good deal. Hurry back and you'll probably find us still at the table near the north wall. I'll watch for you."

Vonnie rammed her arms into her jacket sleeves as she watched Hannah hurry on toward the lunch room. She walked home as quickly as she could. Her mother had mushroom soup and a pear and grated cheese salad waiting for her. It was a frustrating lunch hour. Her mother kept asking questions and Vonnie really wanted to share school happenings with her, yet she couldn't mention her problems about snacktime and lunch hour without her mother pointing out that her troubles were self-imposed, that she could be free of them by letting people know about her diabetes. No way. She told her mother about the English assignment.

"I've read 'The Lottery,' " her mother said. "What do you think the theme is?"

"It's really a sad story, I think. And a scary story, too, in a way. It seems to me that the author is saying that people really don't care what bad things happen in the world unless those bad things are happening to them."

"That is scary," her mother admitted.

"Do you think that's a universal truth? That's what Miss Biskis said we were to look for."

"Miss Biskis doesn't want my opinion. You'll have to discuss the story theme with Allison."

"I suppose so." Somehow Vonnie thought Allison wasn't really going to be interested, but maybe she was wrong.

She hurried back to school, but by the time she had gone to her locker to hang up her jacket, by the time she got out her textbooks for the afternoon, the three-minute warning bell rang and there was no time to meet Hannah and her friends.

Art class dragged because she wasn't quite sure what was expected of her. Miss Bell asked to see some samples of her work and she had nothing with her. She would bring some sketches on Thursday. She was really interested in art. She might even major in art in college . . . maybe. She hadn't decided for sure.

She was glad when it was time for Spanish. Not only was Spanish her favorite subject, but it also was the last class of the day and she was ready for school to be out. In a way this day had been harder to face than yesterday. She would be glad when it was behind her. At least some of the kids knew now that she ate lunch at home and she had gotten the message across without having to explain. She felt in charge of herself and that made her feel good about herself.

"Sorry I didn't make it back in time to see you in the lunch room," Vonnie said as Hannah sat down beside her at an oak table for four.

"No big deal," Hannah said. "Got your translation finished?"

Vonnie pulled her homework from her notebook and opened her Spanish text. She liked the Spanish room. It was a small class and four people sat at each table where there was plenty of room to spread out texts and notebooks and paper. But the thing she really liked about the room was the walls. The walls were like colorful pages from an atlas. Mr. Valdez, their teacher, had hung maps of all the countries where Spanish was spoken. She hadn't been surprised at seeing Spain and Mexico and Central America. She had been surprised that Brazil had been blacked out on the map of South America until she realized that Portuguese was the official language in Brazil.

"Hey, Hannah!" Vonnie nudged Hannah and pointed to a map to their left. "That's Florida!"

"Sure. Lots of people in Florida speak Spanish. Lots of Cubans have come to Florida, people like Mr. Valdez."

"We're lucky to have him for a teacher, aren't we? He really knows what he's talking about."

"In Spanish he does." Hannah giggled. "Sometimes his English is a bit garbled. But I like him and learning to speak Spanish is important to me."

"Why?" Vonnie looked at Hannah with new interest.

"I want to be a nurse some day. I'm a Candy Striper now, and sometimes Spanish-speaking people come to the hospital. There are only two nurses who know enough Spanish to help them. I'd like to be able to help them too. Being able to speak Spanish would make me a more valuable nurse."

"Neat, Hannah. I wish I were that sure about what I want to do after high school. Sometimes I think everyone has his life planned but me."

"Not so." Hannah grinned at her. "I've always

wanted to be a nurse, that's true, but lots of kids haven't made any career choices yet. Of course Allison wants to be an actress and Jeff's decided to go into the family plumbing and heating business, but Chad doesn't have any ideas for the future. And I don't think Pete's very sure of what he wants to do either."

"He said he might study music."

They opened their books and began reviewing the translation one last time. Vonnie was so engrossed that she didn't notice it was Pete who had sat down with them until she heard Hannah speak to him. Then for a moment she held herself very still, not knowing whether to look up and smile or just go on scanning her translation. Again she smelled the clean leather scent that clung to Pete. Was it from the hardware store? she wondered.

"Missed you yesterday," Hannah said.

"I thought of you here conjugating verbs while I was out checking some of the wigglies and squigglies at Ott's pond."

Now Vonnie looked up and smiled. Pete's dimple flashed as he smiled back and he seemed to be waiting for her to say something. He had two black ballpoints clipped to the V-neck of his gray sweater. But why was she noticing such crazy details! He was still looking at her—waiting.

"I wondered why we didn't have any classes together yesterday," she said. "Guess you were on a field trip, right?"

"Right." Pete opened his Spanish book as Mr. Valdez called the class to order.

There was no more time for talking and visiting. Mr. Valdez rapped for attention. He was a tall man.

Middle-aged. Slightly stooped. She couldn't imagine him fleeing across the sea between Cuba and Key West in a rowboat, but that was the story Hannah told her about him. Today Mr. Valdez called on each student to translate one sentence of the assignment. After that they approached new material and each person had to translate one sentence at sight. Vonnie had no trouble. Pete only missed two words. But Hannah broke down completely, having to look most of the words up in the back of the book.

When the dismissal bell sounded Hannah looked as if she had been trying to carry water in a sieve. She groaned in defeat. "I'd be in big trouble if I ever went to Spain."

"Planning a trip?" Pete gave her ponytail a playful tug.

"You never know."

"I'll help you if you want me to, Hannah," Vonnie said. "You just need to drill on vocabulary. Once you get behind it's hard to catch up."

"I could use some help too," Pete said. "Want to start a class? Of course I'd rather take private lessons."

Vonnie felt herself blushing and she knew Pete had noticed. Her face must be fiery red. How could he help noticing! But down deep she liked his teasing. Why couldn't she think of a response!

"She doesn't give private lessons." Hannah wrinkled her nose as she did when she was giving something careful thought. "Not to *you* anyway, Pete. If you get any better you'd change the grade curve and make it harder for everyone to get a decent grade."

"Oh, Hannah's right," Vonnie agreed, finding her

voice at last. "It doesn't pay to coach the competition."

"You girls really know how to flatter a guy." Pete picked up his books and started to walk beside Vonnie as they left the room, but Hannah intruded.

"When are we going to work on that English assignment, Pete? Got any time now? We could sit here for a few minutes and go over some of the basic ideas."

Vonnie held her breath waiting for Pete's answer. How could Hannah be doing this to her! But how ridiculous! Hannah didn't know how badly she wanted Pete to walk to her locker with her. Hannah probably didn't know any crazy lady who fell for a guy after seeing him twice. Or was it three times? Maybe four times by now.

"Can't do it now, Hannah." Pete paused only a moment, then continued walking beside Vonnie. He spoke to Hannah as he glanced at her over his shoulder. "Got to get down to the store. Mr. Johnson has a big winter's end sale on snow shovels. The crowd's probably breaking the door down right now."

How could she be glad and sad at the same time? Her heart was on a teeter-totter, up because Pete was walking with her, down because he had to go right to work.

"That's some English assignment," she said, trying to make some sensible conversation, yet not caring a whit about the English assignment—at least not at the moment.

"Yeah. Old Biskis really dishes out the heavy stuff. But I like her class. It makes me think."

Vonnie was trying to think of another comment.

Why couldn't she just relax and talk to Pete the same way she talked to Hannah or to her parents or . . . Before she could think of anything more to say Pete spoke up.

"How come you don't eat lunch in the cafeteria, Vonnie? I looked for you there today."

"You did?" Vonnie hoped she didn't sound too pleased and she groped in her mind for an answer to Pete's question—an evasive answer. The words flashed in her mind: You don't have to explain; you don't have to explain. But where Pete Karmer was concerned she felt she *did* have to explain—if she wanted him to like her, if she didn't want to appear a snob.

Then her heart rode the teeter-totter again— down because Allison Moore was approaching with a big smile for Pete, up because Allison had already distracted Pete enough to make him forget his question about lunch.

"Hi, Allison. Where are you heading?" Pete asked.

"To talk with you, of course." Allison lowered her lashes, then looked up at him through the sooty fringe. "I've misplaced my English book. Could you let me borrow yours?"

"Then what am I supposed to use?" Pete asked. "You think I've got that story memorized?"

"Well, you have to go to work, don't you?" Allison flung her long golden hair over her shoulders. "I could use your book for a while, then I'll drop it off at the store before you get off work at six."

"Well . . . well . . . okay. But if you forget to drop it off I'll . . ."

"I won't forget, Pete. You can depend on that."

Of course you won't forget, Vonnie thought. What better excuse to see Pete again! She felt prickly as a cactus and she wasn't sure why. Was she irritated at Allison for moving in on Pete? Or was she irritated at herself for feeling so shy and unable to talk with him? Yet what could she have said?

"Ready to go home?" Hannah called as she came hurrying down the hall from her locker at the other end of the building.

"Guess so." Vonnie tried to look at Hannah, but her gaze followed Pete and Allison as they walked off together.

Hannah looked where Vonnie was looking and grinned. "I suppose the blond bombshell swooped him right from under your nose."

"Well, really. We weren't talking about anything important."

"But you like Pete, don't you? I can tell."

"How can you tell?"

"By the way you glared at me when I tried to talk to him about the English assignment."

"Hannah! Really! I didn't glare. I . . ."

"It's okay, Vonnie. Pete and I are just friends. I'm dating Chad right now. If you can make Pete forget Gabrielle, more power to you. He needs something . . . someone."

Vonnie sighed. "You can see that he's walking off with Allison."

Hannah looked directly at her. "No. I don't see that at all. I see Allison walking off with Pete. There's a big difference. And right now Allison is

Jeff's steady. Jeff is Pete's best friend. Pete isn't the kind to shaft a friend."

Vonnie wanted to believe Hannah, but she couldn't quite make her mind to accept Hannah's words. Allison might be walking with Pete, but Pete certainly wasn't beating her off with a stick.

7

After a couple of weeks passed Vonnie's days began to fall into a predictable pattern like spoons nesting in a drawer, each one the same as the next. She arrived at school early enough in the mornings to meet Hannah's friends. Hannah didn't run with the cheerleader bunch, but the kids in her group were nice and friendly and Vonnie enjoyed the casual relationships that resulted from the early-morning gab sessions.

She and Allison turned in their English paper on time, Allison copying most of Vonnie's ideas and suggestions and offering little original thought in exchange. But Vonnie didn't mind a whole lot. She guessed that Miss Biskis knew Allison's ways well enough to figure out who had done most of the work.

Nobody said much to her anymore about going home for lunch. There had been some questions and comments for a few days, but she had managed to handle them with humor and without explaining.

"Your mom must be one terrific cook to get you home every noon," Chad said to her one day as he and Hannah headed for the lunchroom.

Vonnie laughed. "Mom wants to keep me on a diet. She's afraid I'll get fat if I stay at school and eat the heavy 'basketball players' special' that they feed you guys on the team."

"Don't blame *me* for the menu." Chad grinned down at her. "I don't play ball."

"You *don't?*" Was Chad kidding her? She hadn't seen any ball games, but she thought that a guy as big and tall as Chad was would be on the team. She remembered the way Allison had looked up at him, flirted with him. Then she laughed. "You're just putting me on, Chad."

"No way." His smile disappeared. "I had rheumatic fever a couple years back. The doc says no athletics."

She felt heat rush to her face and neck. "I'm sorry, Chad. I didn't know."

"No big deal." Chad twined his fingers through Hannah's as they neared the cafeteria door. "In fact I sort of like having my after-school hours free." He looked down at Hannah and winked.

"And I like it too," Hannah said. "But stop bugging Vonnie about school lunch. I don't blame her for not wanting to eat mystery meat and carrot coins every day. I'd go home too if it made sense. But my mom works and by the time I jogged home, made myself a sandwich and jogged back to school I'd be hungry again."

Vonnie told Hannah and Chad goodbye and walked on home thinking about Chad. He had a heart condition and he didn't care who knew it. He could even see some advantage in it. She knew there weren't any advantages to having diabetes, but she admired Chad's attitude and wished she could be more like him in that respect.

The upcoming weekend was a tough one. Hannah had extra Candy Striper duty. Nobody asked Vonnie to go to the basketball game and she was reluctant to go alone. Her folks helped out by planning dinner and a shopping outing to Crown Center in the city and while it was fun, it wasn't the same as wearing green and gold and going to a basketball game with friends to cheer for the home team.

On the Friday morning of her third week at Roe Village High, Pete came up to her before English class. He was wearing jeans and a blue crewneck sweater that made his eyes look like the sea on a clear day. But the thing she noticed most was the way he was smiling at her. His mouth was full and wide and when his lips curved up at the corners they accented his broad cheekbones. He had never looked so handsome. She smiled because she was wearing jeans and a blue sweater too, because Pete had walked over to her, because they looked like a matched set.

"Are you busy after school this afternoon, Vonnie?"

Her heart leaped up, almost sticking in her throat. She had all but given up hoping that Pete would ever take any real notice of her. He was friendly enough when they met in class or in the halls, but since that second day when he had walked with her to her locker and then gone off with Allison, there had been nothing special between them.

"Can't think of a thing that I really have to do after classes, Pete. What's up?"

"Nothing really." He jammed his hands into his pockets, stretching the blue denim tight across his thighs. "I just thought that if you didn't have plans I'd give you a lift home from school."

"Fine. But don't you have to work today?" She tried to sound casual, not too eager, yet pleased.

"Sure I have to work, but not until three-thirty and we're out early today so the teachers can get to some meeting in the city."

"I forgot all about that. Sure, Pete. I'd like a ride home."

"See you then." Pete grinned and walked over to where Jeff and Chad were standing, their broad shoulders still hunched a bit against the early morning chill. Was there a bit of a strut in Pete's stride? She wondered if he had been afraid of a turn-down.

"What's with *you?*" Hannah asked, joining Vonnie and studying her in surprise. "You look like you're lost in another world."

For a moment she stared at Hannah in her rusty orange slacks and sweater that almost exactly matched her hair, then she found her voice. "Maybe I'm dreaming." The words came out louder than she intended and she lowered her voice. "Hannah! Pete just asked to drive me home from school this afternoon."

Hannah rolled her eyes. "I'm impressed. What's the occasion?"

"I don't know. Oh, well, a teachers' meeting. I mean we get out early because of the teachers' meeting and he has an extra half-hour before he has to report for work."

The bell rang before Hannah could do more than nod her approval at the news and for the rest of the morning Vonnie floated in another world. Her body went to English class and history class as usual, but that was just reflex action. She hardly knew what was going on. Pete had asked to drive her home! And it was because they got out early. Maybe he would have driven her home every day if he hadn't had to work. Maybe that was all that had been keeping him from asking her out—his job. Then she had to remind herself that he really hadn't asked her out. They were merely going to ride home from school together.

Should she ask him in when they reached her house? They could have a soda. Would he ask why she drank diet soda? She was borrowing trouble. Why would he ask a thing like that? Lots of people drank diet soda. But she decided not to invite him in. He might think she was being too forward. Or he might be shy about meeting her mother or . . . Her thoughts were like confetti, whirling and scattering and littering her mind.

On the way to Spanish class she reminded Hannah again. "Don't wait for me after school this afternoon, okay?"

"I'll remember." Hannah flipped her ponytail over her shoulder. "This will be a first, you know."

"The first time we haven't walked home from school together?" She felt a bit puzzled. Was Hannah going to have hurt feelings?

"No. The first time Pete has asked any girl to go anywhere since . . . since . . ." Hannah wrinkled her nose, but she didn't have to finish the sentence. Vonnie finished it for her.

". . . since Gabrielle?"

"Right. I think every girl in school has given Pete the eye, but he's just ignored all the attention and spent all his spare time either practicing on his trumpet or working at the hardware store."

"The trumpet? I didn't know Pete played the trumpet."

"Sure. He's in Jazz Band I and so are Chad and Jeff. Chad's the drummer and Jeff plays piano."

"But when do they practice? I've never heard a jazz band and there's music drifting from the music room all day long."

"Jazz band meets on Tuesdays and Thursdays before school. We're always outside then. You can't hear them from the front of the school. I wonder if Allison knows."

"I suppose she does if Jeff plays in it."

"Not about jazz band, silly, about you and Pete."

"There's really not all that much to know. He's just going to drive me home from school." She tried to make it sound casual, but she knew and she knew Hannah knew, that Pete's invitation was a breakthrough for both of them. It could be the beginning of something very nice.

"Gosh, Hannah. I hope I say the right things. I mean, I hope I can think of *something* to say. What if I just sit there like a stump?"

"Maybe Pete appreciates quiet girls." Hannah giggled.

"What was Gabrielle like? I mean, beside being beautiful, what was she really like?" Self-consciously Vonnie ran her fingers through her Dutch bob, then smoothed it down.

"How did you know she was beautiful?"

She didn't try to squirm out of answering. "I looked her picture up in the yearbook. She was beautiful."

"Yeah, she was, but . . ."

Hannah didn't get to finish the rest of her sentence. Pete strode into the classroom and sat down in his usual place at their table. Vonnie smiled at him, then looked away self-consciously.

76

She thought Spanish class would never end. Mr. Valdez went around the room three times asking each person to translate, then he gave them a long weekend assignment that had everyone groaning. But the bell rang at last and Pete walked with Vonnie to her locker as if he had always walked with her to her locker. She liked having him at her side. It made her feel very special—very special.

"Hi, Pete," Allison called as Vonnie lowered her head to peer at her combination lock. "Got a big weekend planned?"

"Big enough. You too?"

"Jeff and I are going to the early movie. Want to join us?"

Vonnie felt her hackles rise. How could Allison stand there in her *very* green shoes and invite another boy to join her and her boyfriend on their date! She hardly moved while she waited for Pete's answer.

"Sorry, but not tonight, Allison. Got to work. Got other plans."

Vonnie breathed again. She shoved her books into her locker, pulled out her jacket and turned to face Pete. "Ready?"

"Let's make tracks."

"Need to go to your locker?"

"Naw." Pete grinned. "I'll just take these books home and do a little studying over the weekend."

She could feel Allison staring at them as they walked down the hall and she felt very conspicuous. In fact, everyone seemed to be staring at them. Staring and whispering. She could imagine what they were saying: Look! He's with Vonnie Morrison. Where do you suppose they're going? Do you think he's been dating her? But he'll never forget Gabrielle. Never.

"What's the matter, Vonnie? You look so . . . so strange."

She smiled quickly. "Nothing's wrong, Pete." Then she laughed uneasily. "It's just that I feel everyone staring at us."

"So let them stare." He grinned down at her. "Who cares?"

"Right. Who cares!"

Pete led the way to the parking lot and to a tan Chevrolet sedan that was rusting through at the fenders. He opened the door for Vonnie and closed it when she was seated. After he slid beneath the wheel and drove from the lot he put a Bee Gees tape on the tape deck and turned the volume low so they could talk. But she couldn't think of anything to say. The car was big and old and it smelled like wet wool. If it had been black it could almost have doubled as a hearse. But she couldn't say that.

"Neat car, Pete," she blurted at last.

"I bought it from Dad. He was going to trade it in on his new Citation, but there's not much demand for big gas guzzlers anymore. They wouldn't give him much for it, so I bought it. I've tinkered with it some and it gets fair mileage."

Silence. She listened to the Bee Gees, listened to the tires hum against the blacktop. What could she say now? "Roe Village is a pretty town, isn't it?" She looked at the cottages that lined either side of the street like white packages, some big, some small, all differently shaped.

"Yeah, I guess Roe is pretty at that. After you've

lived here all your life you sort of look at it without really seeing it."

Where were they going? Pete seemed to be driving aimlessly, circling a block here, another block there.

"Would you like to stop somewhere for a Coke?" he asked at last.

"If you would," she said. "But do you have time? I don't want to make you late for work."

"It might crowd things a bit." Pete grinned at her and began driving toward her house. "Glad you understand, Vonnie. I have to give up a lot of things for that job, but it's important to me. I'm saving for college. My folks are helping my brother through school and they'll help me too, but I've got to help myself as much as I can."

"I had a job in Washington. I worked in a flower shop. I'll get a job here too this summer. But my folks thought I shouldn't try to work until I was settled in school and all."

"Yeah. It must be really tough to have to move in the middle of the school year."

"I'm used to it. We've moved a lot." Now Pete was parking in front of her house and she hated to see their time together running out. Pete was easy to talk to once she had relaxed. "Hannah tells me you play trumpet in the jazz band."

"Sure do. We're having a big clinic and concert in May and Mr. Claribone is working our tails off getting us ready for it."

"Clinic?"

"Sure. A special one-day learning session. Bick Vane, a trombonist and composer from the west coast is flying here to give us professional tips on improving our techniques. He'll be the soloist with the band at an evening concert."

"Sounds neat."

"It will be. I'm really looking forward to it. Bick Vane's played with the Maynard Fergeson band and now he's composing and doing studio work in L.A. That's what I'd like to do some day—be a professional musician." Pete glanced at his watch. "Vonnie, would you like to go out for a burger and a Coke tonight? I mean it's no really big deal. I have to work until nine because Mr. Johnson is having his annual promotion on gardening supplies. But I could pick you up around nine and we could stop by That Place."

"What place?"

"That Place." Pete laughed. "That's the name of it. It's just a spot where the high school crowd goes on the weekends after games or after the early movie. How about it?"

"Sure, Pete. It sounds great."

"Good. I'll stop by for you a little after nine, okay?"

"Okay. I'll be ready."

Pete opened the car door for her and walked with her up to the porch before he said goodbye. She stepped inside quickly, then she watched until his car turned the corner and disappeared from sight.

Pete Karmer had asked her for a date! Pete Karmer was going to take her to the hangout where all the kids went!

"Mom! Hey, Mom!" She called up the stairway as she began taking the steps two at a time, not stopping until she reached the attic where the smell of turpentine reigned supreme and where her mother was cleaning her paintbrushes. The dormer roof sloped sharply and she ducked her head until she reached the middle of the area where she could stand up straight.

"Vonnie! What's happened?" Her mother stood and wiped her hands on a paint rag, then on her paint-streaked smock. "Something good, I suppose, or you wouldn't be showing me such a jack-o'-lantern grin."

"Pete Karmer asked me to go out tonight, Mom. He's really a neat guy. All the girls are ape over him and he asked *me* to go out." It took a moment for her to realize her mother wasn't smiling.

"Who is this boy, Vonnie? Where are you going with him?"

"Pete Karmer. I told you his name. He's a junior. He's in two of my classes. He works after school at the hardware store. Oh, Mom. He's the boy Dad was teasing me about that first Saturday we went shopping together."

"And where are you going?"

"You're not going to say no, are you?" She felt a creeping coldness deep inside herself. "He asked me to go to That Place—that's the name of the spot—That Place, for a burger and a Coke after he gets off work tonight."

"We'll have to talk it over with your father," her mother said. "We'll see what he says. Let's go downstairs now. I'm through up here for the day."

Now she walked slowly down the narrow steps ahead of her mother. It hadn't occurred to her that she needed to ask permission to go out with Pete. But she knew why. It was because of her determination to keep her secret. Why had she said they were going out for burgers and Coke? She would have to reassure her mother that she wouldn't eat French fries, that she would order a diet soda. But there was no use arguing her cause now. She would wait until her father got home from work. It would give her time to think and plan. Her parents simply couldn't say no.

8

Vonnie felt as if her body were a hollow shell, ice-frosted on the inside, as she waited in the living room for her father to come home from work. She wanted to present her reasons for going out with Pete before her mother had a chance to present her reasons for not wanting her to go. When her father finally arrived he loosened his bronze-colored tie and took off his brown coat as he listened to her.

"The tall dark-haired boy from the hardware store, huh? Nice looking kid. Clean cut. I liked him."

Her father's blue eyes held a friendly brightness as he looked at her and she felt a breath of warmth touch her inner chill.

"Then you mean it's okay for me to go out with him tonight?"

"Well, now let's think about that a minute." Her father draped his jacket over his left arm, loosened his shirt collar and looked at his wife who had just joined them. "Does Pete know about your diabetes?"

She looked at the floor. "No, Dad. He doesn't. And I'm not ready for him to know. Not just yet."

"I don't like the risk you're taking by not telling him." Tiny fan-shaped lines deepened at the corners of her mother's mouth as she pressed her lips together, giving her whole face a pinched look.

"Mom, please! If I tell one person then the word will be all over school by Monday morning. We're just going out for a soda. No big deal. I can handle it. I'll probably be home within a couple of hours at the most."

"But if you're planning to be going out with this boy, he should know, Vonnie. Being secretive is as unfair to him as it is to you."

"I don't know whether I'm going to be going out with Pete again or not," she said. "But more than likely it will be *not* if he finds out that I'm . . . different."

"If he's as nice and understanding as you say he is, there should be no problem," her mother said.

"I think I'd rather stay home than tell him." She felt her throat grow tight, but she was determined not to cry as she turned and started upstairs.

"Where did you say you were going, Vonnie?" her father asked.

"To That Place. It's a spot where the kids go. It's across the street west from the courthouse."

"Maybe we can make a deal," her father said. "You can go if you'll promise to call us if you decide to leave That Place and go somewhere else. I know how it is. You'll start out there, then someone will have an idea of a better spot. Just promise to call and let us know if you go to a different place. We want to know where you are."

"And you will be home before midnight, of course," her mother said.

"Fair enough." Vonnie hugged her parents. At

this point she would have agreed to almost anything in return for the privilege of going out with Pete. "I'll call you if we leave That Place and I'll be home before midnight."

"That's just the deal for this time, Vonnie," her father said. "If you're going to start dating, and I really hope you are, you're going to have to let your friends know how to help you in case of an emergency."

"Sure, Dad. Sure." She hated thinking about it. Just for now she wanted to be the girl with no special problem, with no special worry more important than deciding what to wear tonight on the date with Pete Karmer.

She made a Spanish omelet and tossed a salad for their supper, then washed the dishes, glad to have something to do to help her occupy her time until nine o'clock. Thank goodness her parents hadn't fussed about Pete being so late to pick her up. At least they understood about that. After the kitchen was in order she went to her room and stood before her closet trying to decide what to wear. Then, after considering several different outfits she decided to wear what she had on. Pete wouldn't have time to change. He was coming to pick her up right from work. He'd still be wearing his jeans and crewneck and she rather liked their accidentally matched outfits.

She thought he would never arrive. She freshened her makeup. Nine o'clock. Nine-o-five. She brushed her hair again. Nine-o-seven. Should she wait in her room? Or should she go downstairs? No use to try to pretend she wasn't ready. Acting hard to get wasn't her style. And anyway Pete could see from her outfit that she hadn't been spending time getting dressed.

At eight minutes after nine she heard Pete's car stop at the curbing and she ran downstairs. So what if he thought she was eager. She was, wasn't she? And he would feel more at ease if she greeted him first rather than her parents. Loboy was at the door before she could open it, sniffing and prancing.

"Hi, Pete. Come on in and meet my folks."

Pete stepped inside, bent to pat Loboy, then followed her into the living room where she performed the introductions. That's what introductions always seemed like to her—an on-stage performance. But Pete managed his end of the dialogue nicely, smiling and saying the right things. He's used to meeting the public, Vonnie thought. Sales clerks have to know what to say to people.

"Are you getting settled in your new job, Mr. Morrison?"

"Pretty much," her father answered. "And we're enjoying the Midwest."

"I understand you're an artist, Mrs. Morrison."

"I paint some," her mother said.

"She's really good," Vonnie spoke up. "I'll get her to show you some of her landscapes sometime."

"But not tonight," her mother said. "You two run along now and have a good time."

"Nice to meet you." Pete smiled at both of her parents before he and Vonnie turned and went out the front door.

Vonnie relaxed after she got into the car and they headed toward town. She hadn't really been holding her breath, yet suddenly her lungs felt like deflated balloons and she sank back against the car seat. Her parents had liked Pete. She could tell.

"You've got nice folks, Vonnie."

"I think so. But sometimes they're awfully strict."

"I guess every kid thinks that about his parents." Pete laughed. "At least I think mine are strict too sometimes."

"What are they strict about?"

"Oh, stuff like grades and saving money and getting enough sleep and not eating junk food and . . ."

She giggled. "They sound just like my folks. Honestly. They do. Maybe they all get it from a book. You know, chapter one . . . worry about grades. Chapter two . . . worry about money for college. Chapter three . . ." She stopped. She didn't want to discuss health matters with Pete. Not now. Not tonight. Maybe not ever.

Vonnie grew tense again as Pete parked the car in the courthouse parking lot and they walked toward That Place. Who would be inside? She hoped she would know some of the kids. Would she and Pete join a group? Or would they sit alone? She knew everyone who knew Pete would be watching them and speculating on what he saw in the new girl.

The narrow-faced building had a buff brick exterior, two round windows like small eyes on either side of the door and a neon sign above the entry which spelled THAT PLACE in blue lights. The door was closed and when Pete pushed it open, a rock tune blared from the juke box and the smell of frying hamburger wafted into the air.

The room was fairly well lighted and Vonnie tried to see everything in one glance, tried not to appear to be studying it the way a first-timer might. Scarred pine booths lined the two side walls, round oak tables and straight-backed chairs dominated the center of the room and toward the back across from the kitchen a red jukebox and a red-tiled floor provided a place for dancing. Covers from hit albums decorated the walls and here and there foil-covered music symbols, suspended from the ceiling, shimmered in the flash of a strobe light.

Pete reached for her hand, twining his fingers through hers as he headed toward the back of the room. His touch gave her confidence. She recognized nobody in the first few booths, but she knew Pete knew all the kids because he smiled and nodded at them and they smiled back.

"Hey, Pete! Over here!"

She looked in the direction of the voice and saw Jeff rising from a booth and waving to Pete. Then Chad peered at them from over the back of the same booth, his red hair making Jeff's brown hair seem dull by comparison.

"Shall we join them?" Pete asked. "They've saved us a place. You know Allison and Hannah."

"Sure." She didn't elaborate on what her "sure" meant. Sure she wanted to join them or sure she knew the girls. Pete obviously wanted to be with his friends. When they reached the booth the other four scooted over to make room for them. She sat down beside Jeff and across from Hannah and Chad, and Pete sat beside Chad across from her. And across from Allison and Jeff. Then everyone was silent. She could sense the kids in the other booths glancing at them, whispering about them. It was like going to school on the first day again. It was like walking from the schoolhouse with Pete this afternoon. And to add to her unease she noticed that the girls had changed clothes. Tonight Hannah had on a neat brown outfit, slacks and a cable knit sweater. And Allison was wearing lemon-colored cords and a matching shirt. Green shoes? Vonnie could hardly keep from looking at Allison's feet.

"Why didn't you tell us you were coming here?" Jeff asked Pete. "We just got out of the movie. We could have saved a table if we'd known you were coming."

"Table—schmable." Pete laughed. "There's plenty of room right here, isn't there?"

"Sure. Sure." Chad answered. "Plenty of room if we make like sardines."

Vonnie smiled at Hannah who seemed glad to see her, but Allison was looking at Pete, smiling at Pete in that special way of hers. And Pete was smiling back. But what was wrong with that! She wished she could relax around Allison. And she wished she could think of something to say. They would really think she was stupid if she just sat around like a wart on a toad. But just then the waitress arrived, bringing a tray of burgers, fries, Cokes.

"Mine's the tall Dr. Pepper." Hannah reached for her drink as the waitress set the things on the table. The oniony fragrance of the sandwiches made Vonnie's mouth water.

"Would you two care to order?" the waitress asked, looking from Pete to Vonnie.

"What would you like?" Pete asked her.

"Just a diet Pepsi, please."

"Better have a burger," Pete urged. "I'm starved."

"But you're a working man. I'll just have the Pepsi, I think. I'm really not hungry."

"Then make it one light Pepsi, a tall Coke and a burger," Pete told the waitress.

"I wish I had your willpower," Hannah said to

Vonnie. "I'm the one who needs to turn down the burger and fries."

"Why should anyone turn them down?" Allison asked. "Someone's always trying to stamp out the fun things."

Vonnie felt like a wet blanket until Jeff spoke up.

"Aw, come on, Allison." He poked her playfully. "Nobody's trying to spoil your fun."

"And they'd better not either," Allison said. She leaned forward to sip her Coke, letting her shining hair fall over her shoulder and brush against Jeff's arm. It looked like cornsilk against his navy blue shirt.

"Hey, listen to that tune," Hannah said. "That's a number you guys play in jazz band, isn't it?"

"Yeah, man. It is at that." Chad began to beat out the rhythm on the edge of his Coke glass, using his straws like drum sticks. "Think we'll ever sound that good?"

"We might," Pete said. "Some day."

"Pete, you sound just as good as that trumpet player." Allison looked into Pete's eyes. "You really do. I can't tell any difference at all."

"The vibrato on the ballad section is different." Jeff said. "Can't you hear that?"

"I like Pete's vibrato a lot better," Allison said. "It's . . . smoother."

Jeff took a big bite of his sandwich, then Chad spoke again. "Let's go back to the jukebox and see if there's any more tunes that we play. It's neat to hear how a real pro interprets and improvises. We might come up with some ideas and surprise Mr. Claribone."

Pete stood and Chad joined him. Vonnie got up and let Jeff out. Then she sat back down again as the boys left. She didn't mind being left with Hannah, but there was something about Allison's presence that made her feel as if she had intruded, or as if she had just opened a door that was clearly marked private. And again she could think of nothing to say. Now was no time to talk about school work or assignments. The basketball season had ended, so there was no game to talk about. She took another sip of her drink.

"How can you stand that stuff?" Allison asked. "I think it tastes like soapsuds."

"I like it," Hannah said before Vonnie could reply. "Mom always keeps it for me at home."

"How come you aren't drinking it here then?" Allison asked sarcastically.

"Sometimes I like variety," Hannah said.

"I really go for the decorations in here." Vonnie tried to change the subject. "Sometimes we just take record jackets for granted without realizing how much thinking and planning and art work goes into them."

"That's really true, isn't it?" Hannah said. "Just look at the colors and the designs and the lettering."

"How'd you manage it, Vonnie?" Allison asked, not bothering to look at the walls or to comment on the decorations.

"Manage what?" Vonnie asked. "If you mean noticing the album covers, it's probably because I'm really interested in art and . . ."

"You know I'm not talking about the decorations *or* about art. How did you manage to get Pete to tumble?"

"I didn't *manage* it at all." She tried not to bristle at Allison's insinuation that she had trapped Pete. "He just asked and I just said yes."

"I think it's great," Hannah said. "I mean Pete's kept to himself long enough. It's time he got back into circulation again, time he started having a good time once in a while instead of just going to school and working and practicing and . . . Well, you know how he's been these last months . . . like a snail in a shell."

"Maybe he found out Vonnie is a cheap date." Allison looked pointedly at the diet Pepsi. "Most guys get nicked a little more than for a diet cola."

"Allison!" Hannah scowled. "I'm sure Pete didn't ask Vonnie what she was going to order ahead of time. What's the matter with you anyway?"

"Oh, I'm just kidding," Allison said. "Can't you take a joke? I know Vonnie must have lots of hidden talents."

Vonnie eased her forefinger around the neck edge of her sweater, knowing she was blushing furiously. She wished she could get up and walk away, but she could hardly do that. Where would she walk to? The ladies' room, maybe. But that would be obvious and she didn't want Allison to know she had bothered her that much by anything she had said.

"I think it's great you've hit it off so well with Pete," Hannah said.

"And I suppose you think he's forgotten all about Gabrielle," Allison said, "just because a new girl has hit town."

"No. None of us will ever forget Gabrielle, will we?" Hannah took another sip of her Dr. Pepper. "I know I wouldn't want to forget her and I'm sure Pete wouldn't either. But there's a difference between remembering and clinging to the past like ivy to stone. I'm glad Pete's ready to notice a new face."

The boys were strolling back from the jukebox, but before they could sit down again Allison spoke up. "Why don't we dance a few numbers?" She was easing Vonnie from the booth before anyone could agree or disagree.

Again Pete took Vonnie's hand and the warmth of his touch counteracted some of Allison's coldness. Chad fed the jukebox some quarters and the six of them began to dance. Vonnie had worked out a few steps and she tried them now, feeling a little self-conscious as she let herself glide and turn to the rhythm of the tune. It was during the second number that Allison moved in closer. And closer. At last it seemed as if she were dancing with Pete rather than with Jeff. When that tune ended they all hovered around the jukebox and when the music started again, Allison took Pete's hand and pulled him back onto the dance floor.

"Teach me that last step you were doing, Pete. It's really neat."

Pete hesitated a moment, looking at Vonnie. "You don't mind, do you, Vonnie?"

"Go ahead. We'll all take notes." She kept her voice light, but it griped her that Allison could lead Pete off so easily and in a way that would make her look like a sorehead if she protested. She watched as Pete began the steps again, shoulders up, then down, knees bent, then straight, fingers pointing to the ceiling then to the floor. Allison danced beside him, mimicking his movements, laughing up at him when she made mistakes.

"She catches on quickly," Hannah said in admiration as she tried to mimic a few of Pete's steps from where she stood on the sidelines.

"She's a fast study all right." Sarcasm dripped from Jeff's voice. When the tune ended and Pete and Allison left the dance floor, Jeff glared at Allison.

"Let's go, Al. Get your things."

"It's early," Allison said coolly. "It's not even eleven o'clock. You got a curfew or something?"

Jeff's face flushed but he didn't back down. "I'm leaving. Now."

"Well, I'm not," Allison said. "See you around." She thumped back down in the booth, and Vonnie felt wary as she saw Chad and Hannah hesitating to join her. For a moment she thought Pete was going to slide into the booth beside Allison, but he didn't.

"Maybe it's time we all went somewhere else," Pete said. He looked at Jeff's back as Jeff walked out the door and his expression told Vonnie that he wished he could go after Jeff and bring him back.

"Let's buzz out to the Teepee," Allison suggested. "I think there's a live group playing out there on weekends."

"No way," Hannah said. "That's off limits for me."

"Me too," Chad agreed.

"I don't believe you guys," Allison said.

"Maybe it's just time we went home," Pete said.

"Maybe so," Vonnie agreed, not blaming Jeff for being mad, but irritated at Allison for spoiling her first date with Pete. No. That wasn't right. Allison couldn't spoil things for her unless she allowed her to and she wasn't going to allow it. She looked up at Pete. "It's been fun, but I'm ready to go anytime you are."

"We'll drive you home, Allison," Chad offered.

Allison sighed and pouted prettily. "I don't want

you to have to go out of your way. Pete will be going right by my house after he takes Vonnie home."

"And so will Chad," Hannah said. "Come on, Allison. You're riding with us tonight. We'll drop you off right now."

Vonnie could have hugged Hannah because now Pete was taking her hand again, heading toward the door, while Hannah had linked her arm through Allison's and was keeping her between herself and Chad like the filling in a sandwich. It wasn't until they were outside and in Pete's car that he spoke again.

"I'm sorry about what happened, Vonnie. Sometimes Allison and Jeff don't get along too well and it sort of spoils things for everyone."

"It's all right, Pete. I really had a good time and I think That Place is neat."

"I hope you're saying you'll go there with me again sometime."

"I'd like that."

"So would I." He squeezed her hand. They drove in silence for a ways with Pete taking a roundabout route home. When at last he parked the car at the curbing in front of the old Victorian house he turned to face her, relaxing against the back of the seat and the car door as if he were in no hurry to get out, in no hurry to end their evening.

"I'd like to know what went on tonight, Vonnie."

"What do you mean?"

"I'm not sure exactly what I mean. Allison's always been a big flirt and Jeff knows it. Sometimes I think he kind of likes it—makes him feel special because she could go out with anyone, yet she's chosen him—that sort of thing. But tonight was different. I felt undercurrents I didn't understand. She's never come on quite so strong to me before. I don't blame Jeff for getting ticked off, but I don't want him mad at me. What did you girls talk about while we were back at the jukebox?"

"Nothing special that I remember."

"Well, think, will you? I'm going to have to talk to Jeff about what happened tonight and I'd like to know for sure where I'm coming from."

Suddenly Vonnie felt very wary. What she said now could either draw Pete to her or it could turn him off completely. But why was she so uneasy! Her only choices were to refuse to answer or to tell the truth. She opted for the latter.

"Hannah and Allison were talking about you, Pete, about how nice it was that you were . . . were going out again . . . after, well . . . after Gabrielle and all."

"And what did you say to all that?" Pete's voice was tight and a bit high-pitched.

"I didn't say much. What could I say? You can't think that I hadn't heard about . . . Gabrielle, can you? It's really very sad. I know how you must feel about her. I'm so sorry. And I do understand. I want you to know that."

"I'm sure you do. I thought . . . hoped that perhaps you were different."

Vonnie couldn't believe the coldness that frosted Pete's voice. What had she said to make him so angry? She couldn't imagine. Yet he flung open the car door, jumped out and now he was jerking the passenger door open. She eased from the seat and started toward the house, but no matter how fast she walked Pete was two steps ahead of her. When they reached the door he turned abruptly.

"Good night, Vonnie." And he was gone.

She wanted to call after him, to stop him. Yet she could think of nothing to say: Come back? I had a great time? I want to apologize? But what did she have to apologize for! She could hardly believe the evening had ended so horribly. She knew Pete would never call her again.

9

A soft golden light glowed from a table lamp in the living room and Vonnie snapped it off before she started upstairs. She hoped her parents were asleep and wouldn't hear her, yet she knew that was too much to wish for. The stair treads creaked and the hall light shone into their bedroom doorway.

"That you, Vonnie?" her mother called as she reached the top of the stairs.

"Yes. I locked the door and turned out the living room light." Any other time she might not have minded sharing details, but tonight after the way Pete had acted, she wanted to keep her thoughts and her feelings to herself.

"Did you have a good time?" her father asked.

Vonnie stepped to her parents' doorway to reassure them that she was all right. "Yes, we had a good time." That was the truth. They had had a good time, for a while at least. "I drank a diet Pepsi and that was all."

"Was it a nice place?" Her mother's voice sounded drowsy.

"Yes. It was really okay. I'd like to go back again sometime. There were booths and tables and a jukebox and a dance floor. We met Hannah and

98

Chad and Allison and Jeff Jenks. Jeff's Pete's best friend." Or at least he was until tonight, she thought.

"Sounds like a nice group," her mother said. "Better get to bed now. We'll see you in the morning."

She prepared for bed knowing she wouldn't be able to sleep, yet she did sleep and it was past nine o'clock when she opened her eyes to the east light playing against her yellow walls. She lay in bed for a while enjoying the soft warmth of the sheets and quilt as she thought about her date with Pete, threading the memory through her mind like a film. Everything had been fine until the moment she had told him they had talked of him and Gabrielle. What had she said that had been so terrible? She let Pete's words replay in her brain, wondering what he had meant: *I hoped that perhaps you were different.* In what way had he hoped she was different? Different from whom? Hannah? Allison? Gabrielle? She certainly was different from all three of them.

All day Saturday she thought Pete might call to apologize, or maybe just call to talk. But the phone was silent. She lifted the receiver once to see if the line was dead, but it hummed. She scowled. She wanted to call Hannah and tell her what had happened, yet she hesitated to discuss such a private matter. She liked Hannah, but she had no real assurance that Hannah was close-mouthed. Hannah might tell just one other best friend and that person might tell just one more until the story was all over school.

On Sunday she knew Pete wasn't going to call and on Monday she dreaded going to school. She felt somehow responsible for the rift between herself and Pete, yet she still couldn't pinpoint exactly what she had done. She knew she should have kept her mouth shut about Gabrielle. That was clear enough. She walked to school with Hannah, but their conversation merely skimmed the surface of her thoughts and failed to touch on the true problem bothering her.

"You and Pete have a good time Friday?"

"Yes, but I hated it that Allison and Jeff broke up."

"Oh, don't worry about that." Hannah's orangy ponytail swung as she walked along. "They go at it every now and then, but they always make up."

"And Pete and Jeff? I'd think there would be some hard feelings there."

"Those guys both understand Allison, Vonnie. She may be a mystery to you, but we've grown up with her. I guess you could say we understand her *and* her folks. They baby her. They've brought her up to believe that her wish is everybody's command."

"But why?"

"Oh, they're a lot older than most of our folks— almost old enough to be her grandparents. Mom says they thought they weren't going to have any kids, so when Allison came along they were so pleased they spoiled her rotten. The guys know she's a brat."

"But a beautiful brat. I suppose that makes a difference."

"Yeah. You'll see. She and Jeff will make up over the weekend and Jeff and Pete will still be best buddies."

And Hannah was right. When they reached the schoolhouse Vonnie looked away from the silvery glare of sun on windowpanes and as she turned her head she saw Allison, Pete and Jeff leaning against the red brick of the building, laughing and talking together as if nothing had come between them only a few nights ago. Vonnie stood at the edge of a group of girls, hoping Pete might come over and talk with her. But he didn't.

After the bell rang she got to her seat first in English class and when Pete came in she saw him several seconds before he saw her. His navy sweater and white shirt made his eyes seem very dark blue. Did he look tired? Had he had any trouble sleeping? She guessed not.

"Hi, Pete."

"Hi."

And that was their conversation for the day. Would he have spoken first if she had not? Pete didn't wait to walk with her between classes, and at last period Spanish, he arrived barely in time to sit down before Mr. Valdez called the class to order.

Three separate times on Tuesday Vonnie saw Pete walking with Allison, his dark features contrasting with her fair skin and golden hair. Or was Allison walking with Pete? It was hard to tell, but the end result was the same. They made a handsome study in opposites and everyone who saw them was aware of it. Vonnie knew that Pete had excluded her from his life just as easily as he had included her. Whatever it was that first had attracted them to each other was no more.

"What's the matter?" Hannah frowned, making the freckles between her eyes seem darker than usual as she and Vonnie walked home from school on Tuesday afternoon. "You down about something?"

"Just about Pete. I really bombed out with him Friday night and I don't know why."

"Don't take it personally. I told you that every girl in school's been after Pete and he hasn't given any of them a tumble." Hannah bounced along as if she had springs on her feet, unmindful of Vonnie's lagging steps. "When he asked you out I really thought something might come of it. But your date probably just reminded him of all the good times he'd had . . . in the past."

"I think there was more behind his behavior than that."

"What then?" Hannah tilted her head to one side and looked at Vonnie with interest.

She sighed and decided that it didn't matter what Hannah knew or told. Pete was out of her reach no matter what either of them did or thought. "Pete was really uptight when he left me on Friday night, Hannah. And the worst part of it is that I don't know why."

"What did he say?"

"He asked me what you and I and Allison had been talking about that might have made Allison act as she did. I told him I didn't know, that we had talked of Gabrielle, that I knew about her. I thought it was best to be honest with him."

"And he got mad?"

"He said he had hoped I might be different. I don't know what he meant. I really don't."

"No." Hannah scowled thoughtfully. "I don't either."

"I really like him, Hannah. If there was anything I could do to make things better between us, I'd do it. But I just don't know."

"Yeah. It's a puzzler all right. But Pete's good-natured and he's fair-minded. Maybe he'll come around and level with you one of these days. Don't give up on him."

After she and Hannah parted Vonnie went inside and up to her room. Her mother was out and she was glad to be alone. She flopped onto her bed and stared at the yellow ceiling, feeling like a failure. Maybe her mother was right. In Washington maybe she had been blaming her diabetes for problems that had been in no way related to it. Maybe her inability to keep on friendly terms with Pete, her inability to attract other boyfriends was a personality problem rather than a medical problem. But then, she hadn't really tried to attract any other boys, had she?

Vonnie thought March was the dullest month she had ever experienced anywhere. She had filled in the hours making yellow and white gingham curtains for her room. In April definite signs of spring raised her spirits. Hyacinths popped up on the south side of the house and bloomed in jewel tones of pink, blue, lavendar. The maples and oaks showed pale green buds and in the front yard dandelions began buttoning the sod to the ground. She could smell spring on the damp-earth breezes that began to blow in from the south.

It was at the end of the second week in April that Miss Bell, her art teacher, asked her to report to the art room after school. Vonnie was willing enough. She liked art and she liked Miss Bell with her paint-splattered skirts and chambray work shirts. And her smiling good humor. Miss Bell was short, dark-haired, green-eyed and she smiled in a gentle way that made Vonnie want to do whatever she asked. When she reported that Wednesday after school, Miss Bell came right to the point of their meeting.

"I've chosen you to be in charge of making posters for the music department, Vonnie, because you're exceptionally good at lettering."

"Thank you, Miss Bell." She wished she were good at sketching, at composition, but being good at lettering was a start. She was pleased that Miss Bell had noticed her work. "What are the posters for?"

"They'll promote the jazz clinic and concert that will take place in three weeks. Mr. Claribone would like posters placed in prominent spots in the business district—banks, stores, the courthouse—anywhere where people will notice them, read them."

"How many posters will be needed?"

"Maybe twenty or so." Miss Bell brought white poster board from the supply room and Vonnie smelled the newness of it. "You can recruit helpers if you need to, Vonnie, but I want *you* to plan the master design and rough-sketch it on the posters. After that's done, you can ask other art students to help with the finishing details."

"Where will I work?"

"You can work here after school and before school if you're an early bird. Or you can take the supplies home with you and work there."

"Maybe I could work at home on the weekends and at school during the week."

"That sounds like a reasonable plan."

"How soon do you want me to start on the project?"

"Right away. Today even, if you have the time."

"I might as well get started. Do you have the information that goes on the posters?"

"Mr. Claribone is sending Pete Karmer from the

music department to help get us started. He should be here any minute now. I believe he has to get to a job downtown, so this first meeting shouldn't take long."

Suddenly Vonnie felt so tense she could hardly swallow. It was too late to say no. She had already said yes. And there was no graceful way to tell Miss Bell that she would rather not work with Pete. Anyway, it would be a lie. She would like very much to work with Pete if she could only be on friendly terms with him again.

"Here he is now," Miss Bell said.

Vonnie turned to face Pete as he stepped through the doorway and into the art room. His ranginess always surprised her, yet she knew how tall he was. She had never seen him wear green before. It made his eyes look the color of turquoise—at least they were a blue-green that gave his whole face an undecided look, a look that made her think he would like to turn and run. But of course he didn't do that. She smiled, but he did not return the smile. His wide mouth seemed soft and vulnerable as he looked directly at Miss Bell.

"Mr. Claribone has sent me to help with the jazz clinic posters." Pete reached into his shirt pocket. "I have the information right here." He pulled out a white folded sheet, flattened it and laid it on Miss Bell's desk. She read it carefully.

"This seems complete, Pete. I think we're ready to get to work on the posters whenever you're ready. Have you met Vonnie Morrison?"

"Yes," Pete said. "We've met."

"Good. I've chosen Vonnie to be in charge of the art work on the poster project. You two can make arrangements to get together for an initial meeting. I think both of you should decide on the poster format. Vonnie will offer an artistic viewpoint and you, Pete, can offer ideas that point up sales and ticket promotion. Mr. Claribone will give you some guidance if you need it. Sound okay?"

"Fine," Pete said.

"Good. Then you and Vonnie plan a time for your first meeting. If you'll excuse me for a few minutes I have to take some reports to the office." Miss Bell smiled, then was gone. Vonnie looked at Pete and decided to let him speak first since he was the one involved in jazz band. She was glad Miss Bell had said she had *chosen* her to work on the project. She didn't want Pete to think she had volunteered.

"When would you like to get together, Vonnie? I have to report for work in just a few minutes."

"Whenever it's convenient for you." She remembered his Tuesday–Thursday rehearsals. "How about before school on Friday morning?"

Pete shook his head. "I have to help Dad with the chores. I'm lucky to get here by the time the first bell rings."

"Then you suggest a time."

"What about after supper tonight? We could meet at the library."

"Fine. How about seven-thirty?" She was surprised at the assurance in her voice because she was shaking inside.

"Okay, Vonnie. I'll see you then."

"I'll work out some ideas on this poster board, working in pencil."

"Then you better take this information sheet." Pete started to hand her the paper, but it slipped from his fingers. They both stooped and reached for it at the same time, their hands touching for an

106

instant before Vonnie drew back and let Pete pick it up. She saw a slow flush rise from the green V of his shirt collar to his dark hairline and she knew he felt as ill at ease as she did. She took the information sheet from him, pretending to read it, then nodded.

"Thanks, Pete. See you at the library." This time she was the one to turn and leave. She walked slowly, feeling Pete's gaze upon her back. She really didn't expect him to catch up with her, to walk with her from the school building. And he didn't.

10

Vonnie wondered how she was going to bear working with someone who really didn't want to work with her. Was Pete wondering the same thing? Why did she always feel so insecure? Part of her hoped that Pete would forget whatever it was that had angered him on their Coke date back in February, but another part of her still resented his behavior. The memory of his actions was like a half-healed wound that threatened to open and fester.

"Hi, Vonnie," her mother called from the kitchen as Vonnie slammed the front door a bit harder than she meant to.

"I'm home, Mom." She beelined for the kitchen for her afternoon snack and she could smell roast and onions simmering in the Dutch oven on top of the stove. "Smells good."

"We're eating early tonight." Her mother removed a red checked dish towel which had been tied around her waist as a makeshift apron and poured herself a cup of tea, joining Vonnie as she drank her milk. "Your dad has a special meeting in the city. I may go with him and do some shopping at one of the malls. Would you like to come along?"

"I'd like to, but I can't. Miss Bell put me in charge of making some posters and I have a meeting at the library with Pete Karmer."

"The boy . . ."

"Yeah. He's in jazz band and the posters will advertise a jazz concert."

"How nice that Miss Bell chose you."

"Yeah, I was really pleased about that." No use telling her mother how funny she felt about working with Pete.

"I could stay home if you and Pete want to meet here. I don't have anything special to shop for. We could set up card tables in the attic and you could just leave them there until you finish the project."

"Thanks, Mom, but the library will be fine. This first meeting is just to work up a layout for the posters. After that I'll do some of the work in the art room at school and some of it here at home."

"Fine. But you're welcome to bring your friends here. You know that."

Vonnie went to her room after she finished her snack and penciled a tentative layout on both sides of the poster board. She did three rough sketches on notebook paper—enough to give Pete some choices in the kind of lettering to be used, the position of the words.

What should she wear? Why was that always such a big decision! Deep down she knew she wanted to look nice so Pete would be impressed, so he would notice and remember her. And now that she was going to be with him again she realized that her feeling for him hadn't changed. She had only managed to bury it for a few weeks with the hurt and resentment she had felt following their first date. But this wasn't a real date. She had to remember that. This was just a business meeting arranged by teachers and circumstances.

She decided to wear her jeans and clogs and a pale blue shirt. She wondered if Pete ever wore blue to draw attention to his eyes or if that was just a girl's trick. She pulled her hair behind her ears and held it there with a blue band. That gave her a different look. Surely Pete couldn't help but notice.

Dinner dragged by. She liked the meal well enough, but she was glad when the dishes were cleared and the kitchen was in order.

"Better take the car, Vonnie," her mother said. "Unless Pete is picking you up."

"No, I thought I'd walk." She really didn't want to drive. There was always the chance Pete might bring her home if she were walking.

"I don't like the idea of you walking after dark," her father said, "especially when we'll be out of town. Take the car, okay?"

"Okay, Dad. And thanks."

Her parents left the house first and she did the rest of her homework before she went out. She rolled the car window down so she could enjoy the smells of early spring—the damp earth, the warm moistness of the night air. In the distance she heard a dog barking—a lonesome sound. When she reached the library she looked around for Pete's tan Chevvy, but it was nowhere in sight. She waited. She didn't want to seem too eager for this meeting. Five minutes passed before Pete drove up, parked right in front of the library and sauntered inside. She wondered if he ever hurried. He always seemed so confident, so sure of himself. She waited two more minutes, then went inside, trying to seem as casual as he had.

The April evening was so soft and warm that the library was like a sauna by comparison. In the reading room the yellow table where Pete was sitting contrasted with his dark good looks. Her smile was a reflex as he looked up and spoke to her.

"Hi." She dropped the word between them, then laid the poster board on the table.

"Hey! You've really been working!" Pete sounded businesslike and eager to get going on their project. "Miss Finkle said we could use meeting room 'A' downstairs so we can talk without bothering anyone."

"Good." She picked up the poster board while Pete rose, and they headed for the stairway. The library basement had a dank concrete smell and the "A" room retained the odor of coffee and cigarette smoke from some previous meeting. She laid the poster board on a center table, pulled up an aluminum folding chair and sat down. "Here's what I've done for starters."

Pete pulled up another chair and sat beside her. She guessed he hadn't gone home after work because he still had on the green shirt he had worn to school. He studied both sides of the poster, then looked at the other ideas she had sketched on paper before he spoke.

"You've really done a lot of work since school, haven't you?"

"A couple hours' worth, I suppose." It pleased her that Pete realized that art work and lettering took time. "Which layout do you like best?"

Pete studied the samples thoughtfully. "I really like all of them."

She felt a strong pulse beating in her throat and realized that pleasing Pete had been important to her. "Maybe I could make four or five posters of each type."

"I don't know." Pete studied the samples again. "I think maybe the bold block letters would be the most effective. What do you think? We want to catch peoples' eyes."

"The block letters do have a mass about them that's eye-catching and forceful, I think. Of course color will play a big part in the eye appeal too."

"How about block letters in red on white?"

"You want all the posters the same color?"

"What do you think?"

She felt pleased that Pete seemed genuinely interested in her opinion. "It might be a good idea. If all the posters are alike people may notice them subconsciously as well as consciously. Maybe a little voice inside them will begin to say, 'I saw that sign somewhere else. What's going on?' At least that's what we can hope will happen." *We.* She liked saying *we* to Pete.

"If the posters aren't all alike, then we lose some of the I've-seen-it-somewhere-else effect." Pete nodded. "I think we should make them all alike both in design and in color."

She nodded in agreement. "This is going to be easier than I had thought, Pete. Why don't I make a sample poster to show to Miss Bell and Mr. Claribone? Then if they like it we can go into production right away."

"Sounds good to me. If you can't get enough volunteers from art class to help, I can get some of the kids from jazz band. And the jazz band members will distribute the posters, of course."

"I can get to school early in the morning and work in the art room. I'll want to show Miss Bell a dummy sketch before I begin. She may have some ideas we have overlooked."

"Hope she has a good supply of red poster paint." Pete scraped his chair back from the table. She stood up and began gathering her things. It had been easy to talk to Pete as long as they were talking about the posters. But now she was on edge again and she wanted to end the meeting quickly.

"See you around, Pete. Hope the posters draw a good crowd to your concert." She thought of all the things he might say next: Need a ride home? Are you going to the concert? Would you like to go to the concert with me? But he said none of those things.

"You forgot your ballpoint, Vonnie." He picked it up and handed it to her.

"Oh, thanks." She was about to turn and leave, but the question that had been bothering her for weeks shouted in her mind. "Pete?"

He looked at her questioningly, saying nothing.

"Pete, what did you mean when you said you hoped I was different?" She heard her voice go a bit high and shrill and she tried to lower it. "I mean, I've been thinking about that a lot and . . . and wondering." She looked directly at him, daring him to look away. He accepted the dare, then stared at the floor.

"Forget it, Vonnie. It wasn't important." He slung his jacket over his shoulder, holding it on one finger as he nodded toward the stairs. "Go ahead. I'll snap off the light."

Vonnie hurried from the room, up the stairs and out the front door into the soft night without saying anything more to Pete. What was there to say! She had had a second chance with him and she had blown it. How she envied Allison. And Hannah.

And all the other girls who always seemed to know exactly the right thing to say to boys.

She walked slowly toward her car, realizing Pete wouldn't know whether she was heading toward a car or just toward home. Maybe he would call to her. Maybe he would catch up with her and walk beside her. But neither of those things happened. She got into her car and drove home.

She was glad she had left the living room light on. Its soft glow along with Loboy's barking greeted her when she entered the front hallway. She patted Loboy, then trudged to her room. A bath! Maybe a hot bath would relax her. She ran hot water into the huge, footed tub, added a dash of strawberry-scented bath crystals and soaked in the warm pink froth for over a half hour. She had just toweled herself dry and put on her pajamas when the telephone rang. Her first thought was of her parents. Maybe they had had car trouble. Maybe . . ."

"Morrison residence, Vonnie speaking."

"Hi, Vonnie." Pete's voice flowed across the wire. "Did you realize we forgot to set up a second meeting?"

Pete. It was Pete. He had called her. But it was just a business call. She squelched the excitement that rose inside her. "I didn't think we needed another meeting, but . . ."

"I want to know what Miss Bell thinks about our ideas."

"We could meet in the art room after school for a few minutes."

"Can't take the time then. Mr. Johnson wants me at work the minute school's out. How about eating lunch with me tomorrow, Vonnie. You could tell me what Miss Bell had to say."

Suddenly she realized Pete was going out of his way to see her again. Maybe it was his way of apologizing for his behavior, for avoiding her question at the library. She couldn't refuse. No way.

"All right, Pete. I'll plan to eat lunch at school tomorrow."

"Good deal. I'll see you then."

"Okay." She held the receiver to her ear until she heard the connection break, heard the line humming. Pete had called her! He wanted to see her again! For once she must have done something right. She just wished she knew what it had been.

That night she was asleep before her parents came in, but she told them at the breakfast table about eating at school that noon.

"I don't know, Vonnie. Maybe you could invite Pete here for lunch."

"Oh, Mom. I just can't do that. It would seem . . . pushy. It's really no big deal to eat in the lunch room. I'll watch my diet. I did it all the time in Washington."

"But in Washington your friends knew . . . everyone understood about . . ."

"They knew, *but they didn't understand,*" she said. "I'll be careful what I eat, Mom. There's an a la carte line."

"Okay, Vonnie. But do be careful."

"It's just this once. I won't make eating at school a habit."

She went to school early, made a poster sample for Miss Bell and got her approval of the project. She thought the morning classes would never end, but then when they did, she felt nervous and shy about going into the lunchroom with Pete. She could see kids watching them . . . whispering. She tried to ignore the stares and whispers and to concentrate on other things. This was her first trip to this cafeteria, but she decided there must be a master plan for lunch rooms—big, hard floors, green walls. And they were all like echo chambers, picking up laughter, shouts, the crash of dropped silverware and magnifying the sounds to the pain level. And surely everything that was served had onion in it. At least that seemed to be the dominating fragrance on most days.

"Miss Bell showed the sample poster to Mr. Claribone," Pete said as they balanced brown trays on a stainless steel railing and inched through the cafeteria line. "And he thought it looked great. All conditions are go."

"Hey, that's okay. And guess what! Miss Bell's going to give me extra art credit for this project."

"You deserve it, that's for sure."

"Where shall we sit?" she asked when they had filled their trays.

"The gang's over there at that second table from the wall." Pete headed for the table where Jeff and Allison were sitting with Chad and Hannah.

"Well, look who's here," Allison cooed, glancing at Vonnie. "Did you decide our school lunch wouldn't poison you after all?"

"Here, Vonnie," Hannah said. "I'll scoot over and you can sit by me."

Vonnie sat beside Hannah and Pete sat across from her.

"That all you're eating?" Hannah eyed the milk, the vegetable soup and the banana on Vonnie's tray. "Wish I had that much willpower."

Pete grinned at Hannah. "We wouldn't recognize

you if you weren't working your way through two sandwiches and three desserts."

"I'm just a growing girl." Hannah bit into a peanut butter cookie and washed it down with a sip of Coke.

The longer they sat at the lunch table the more Vonnie felt sure Pete had asked her to eat with him just because he wanted to be with her. He hadn't mentioned the jazz posters again. Yet she still sensed a rift between them, a rift they both were easing around like two colts who had been shocked by an electric fence and didn't intend to let it happen again.

When they finished eating, Pete carried her tray back to the kitchen window. Then he twined his fingers through hers and they walked outside, strolling in the warm April sunshine until the bell rang. She couldn't believe this was happening to her. She hated the intrusion of the bell.

"How about lunch again tomorrow?" Pete asked.

She shook her head. "Thanks, Pete, but my mother is expecting me home."

"She a lonesome lady or something? My mom's glad enough for me to eat school lunch."

Had she blown it again? She chose her words carefully. "Sometimes it's harder for parents to make friends in a new town than it is for kids. Mom sticks to herself a lot." Then she blurted the question that popped into her mind. "Would you like to have lunch with us?"

"Maybe sometime. But not tomorrow."

She was right. She had blown it. Why had she been so pushy! They walked into the schoolhouse and Pete paused beside her at her locker. She looked at all the lockers lining the hall and suddenly they reminded her of coffins standing on end—cold, gray, formidable.

"Vonnie, would you like to go to a movie with me on Saturday night? There's a comedy on in the city, or we could see that suspense film that's playing out at the mall."

Coffins! Was she crazy! Now the lockers were like a row of surprise packages. Who could guess what might be inside! "I'd like to go, Pete. Either movie sounds good."

"I'll pick you up then around seven. Okay?"

"Okay. I'll be ready."

They smiled at each other, then Pete walked on to his locker and she pulled out her books for afternoon classes. Pete had asked her for another date! She could hardly believe it and she could hardly wait until Saturday night.

11

Vonnie waited until Saturday morning when everyone was relaxed and ready to enjoy the weekend before she told her parents about her movie date with Pete. Their reaction to the news was what she had expected. Her father was direct in his comments, but she still had some bargaining power.

"When are you going to tell him?" He was hunched over a second cup of coffee which he had been sipping as he read the sports page of *The Times*.

"I can't tell yet, Dad. Give me just a while longer."

"We'd rather you didn't go into the city for the evening unless Pete knows how to deal with any . . . emergency that might come up."

Silently she hoped Pete wasn't set on seeing the comedy at Ward Parkway, but she didn't let any doubt sound in her tone. "If you don't want us to go into the city, then we'll just see the film that's playing here at the mall."

"I think that would be a good idea." Her mother ran her fingers through her short hair in a way that told Vonnie she was nervous about her date. "And be sure you wear your medallion and chain."

"I always wear it, Mom." She began clearing the breakfast table. "I'll clean up here if you want to paint."

"I have to go to the store," her mother said. "I'll appreciate it if you'll take care of the breakfast things."

The day dragged by. Vonnie did her usual Saturday chores, worked on the jazz posters, took Loboy for a long walk. But no matter what she did her mind kept projecting ahead to the evening. She wondered if Pete was thinking about their date too. She guessed he would be too busy at the hardware store to think much about it.

She shampooed her hair and wished it were longer so she could wear it in a greater variety of ways. She slicked it back behind her ears. No. She had worn it that way the last time she had been with Pete. She combed it smoothly over her ears, fluffing her bangs a bit with the brush. No. She always wore it that way.

"I wish I had a wig," she said as her mother came into her room. "A dozen wigs. Then I could put on a different personality every time I put on my hair."

"And why would you want a dozen different personalities?" Her mother smiled. "The one you have is quite nice, you know."

"You're prejudiced."

Her mother tilted her head to one side and studied her. "You might try a couple of short braids on each side. Or maybe just one on one side. That would be different."

Vonnie combed a section of hair into three strands and tried the idea, wrinkled her nose at the effect and brushed the hair back into her smooth Dutch bob. "Guess I'll just go as the usual Vonnie Morrison."

"You look nice as the usual Vonnie Morrison. I approve." Her mother went on downstairs.

Vonnie wore a blue plaid skirt and a pale blue blouse with a gold pin and was ready when Pete knocked at seven o'clock. He spoke briefly to her parents, then they left in his car.

"You look nice, tonight, Vonnie." Pete pulled away from the curbing and drove toward the highway.

"Thanks, Pete. So do you." She felt herself flush at the stilted exchange of compliments yet she knew hers was sincere and she hoped his was too. Tonight he was wearing tan cord slacks and a brown cord blazer over his tan sport shirt. The earth colors suited him, she thought. Subtle yet very flattering.

"What movie would you like to see?" he asked. "Goldie Hawn's in the one at Ward Parkway."

She made herself look directly at him, hoping for the best. She had promised her parents to stay in town, but Pete needn't know that. She didn't want him to think she was a baby whose parents wouldn't let her go into the city on a date.

"I sure like Goldie Hawn, but I think suspense films are really the most." She hardly breathed as she waited for his response.

"I like suspense stories, too, it's just that . . ."

"What?" Vonnie felt her nails dig into her palms with disappointment that Pete hadn't picked up on her response and agreed on the suspense film. To her surprise she noticed that his face had flushed and his cheeks were the color of ripe plums.

"It's just that Jeff told me he and Allison were

going to the show at the mall. They sort of messed up an evening for us once before and I thought maybe we shouldn't risk letting that happen again."

Vonnie spoke carefully. "Don't worry about that on my account, Pete. It's a big theater and we don't have to sit with them, do we? I'd really like to see that film unless you feel strongly about seeing Goldie Hawn."

Now she was really holding her breath. What was she going to do if Pete insisted on the comedy? She had promised her parents to stay in town . . . or to tell all.

"I'd rather see the suspense film," Pete said. "So let's do it. You're right. We can sit alone."

Vonnie relaxed. She had made it over that hurdle. And when she got to thinking about it she realized she was really pleased that Pete didn't want to sit with Jeff and Allison, that he wanted just the two of them to be together for the evening.

The mall parking lot was jammed and Pete had to leave the car about a block from the theater. There was a florist's stall just inside the mall entrance and Vonnie inhaled the scent of roses and pretended interest in the geraniums and ivies while Pete bought their tickets. But from the corner of her eye she watched for Jeff and Allison. They were nowhere in sight, but she felt edgy as she and Pete entered the dimly-lit theater to choose their seats. The smell of popcorn was like a perfume around them and she was thinking about that when she heard Jeff's voice.

"Hey, Pete!" Jeff turned and called from where he and Allison were sitting in the center section. He pointed to the empty seats next to him. Vonnie watched Allison's face light up with a smile, a smile aimed directly at Pete.

"Mind if I white-lie a little?" Pete whispered.

"That depends." She wondered what he was going to do. They walked on down the aisle until they were even with the row where Jeff and Allison were sitting, then Pete walked over to them.

"You guys are sitting too close to the screen for us," Pete said. "Gives me a headache. We're going to sit farther back."

Jeff shrugged and glanced at the seats behind them. "I like to sit where I can *see,* man."

"Okay. Okay." Pete walked back to Vonnie. "We'll see you later."

Pete took Vonnie's hand, and they walked back about twenty rows. They sat in two empty seats which were surrounded by people. She could see Allison talking to Jeff, then looking back at them and she could imagine the conversation. But she felt safe. Even if Allison talked Jeff into moving, there were no seats really close to her and Pete which they could occupy.

"Want some popcorn?" Pete asked.

"No thanks, Pete." The lights dimmed and "Previews of Coming Attractions" flashed onto the screen as the blare of a trumpet fanfare silenced the hum of voices in the theater. "We got here just in time."

Pete held her hand all through the main feature, grinning at her when she clutched his fingers during the exciting chase scene. She was glad they had come to this theater and she had been so engrossed in the story line that she didn't think about Jeff and Allison until the lights flashed on at the end of the film.

"Another moment of truth," Pete whispered. "We may be stuck with having a snack with them at a drive-in."

"We could go to my house instead," she suggested. "I'll make you a Vonnie Morrison special."

"What's that?"

"It's a secret. I divulge it only within the privacy of the Morrison kitchen."

"Who could resist an invitation like that! Let's duck out of here and get lost in the crowd."

They were closer to the exit than Jeff and Allison were, and easy for them to hurry from the theater and to Pete's car. They left the mall by a rear exit and Vonnie laughed. "I feel like those guys in the movie—fleeing for their lives."

"You sure your folks won't mind us barging in on them like this?"

"They'll be glad to see us. Don't worry about that!" If Pete only knew! Her parents would not only be glad, they would be delighted to have her home where they knew she was safe. And she didn't mind going home as long as Pete was willing. It meant that she could keep her secret a bit longer. She needed to know Pete a lot better before she could tell him. She had to be able to relax around him, to know that he really was her friend. There was still a lot of wariness between them. She felt it and she knew Pete must feel it too.

Her parents looked up in pleased surprise when she and Pete entered the house. "I promised Pete a Vonnie Morrison special, Mom. Okay, if we use the kitchen?"

"Help yourself. We were just going to watch the news before we went upstairs."

She and Pete went to the kitchen and Pete sat down at the old oak table while she began to prepare their snack. Bananas. Peaches, Lemon. Orange. Milk.

"I suppose you have a secret formula that's been passed down through generations of Morrisons." Pete smiled as he watched her plug in the blender.

"Not so. I invented this concoction myself." She didn't add that it consisted of things there were on her special diet. It was a thick drink, delicious and mouthwatering. She poured it into crystal tumblers, then set a plate of crackers in the center of the table for them to munch on.

Pete smiled and rolled his eyes after he tasted the drink. "This really is all right, Vonnie. Do you give out the recipe?"

"Only to very special friends," she teased. She was surprised at how easy it was to relax around Pete when they were alone. Or was it because she was in her own kitchen, her own home? She couldn't hope for an ideal situation like this every time she went out with him. She checked her thoughts. Who said she was going out with him again? Maybe he thought coming home right after the movie was the pits. Maybe he had only been humoring her. But he drank two glasses of her "special" so she knew he wasn't totally turned off by the direction of their evening.

When they finished their snack, Vonnie led the way to the living room. Her parents had gone upstairs. There were two low lights glowing from the corner table lamps, and the TV was tuned softly to a variety show. They sat down on the sofa and watched the program for a few minutes, then Pete took her hand.

"I really do owe you an explanation, Vonnie. I was almost surprised when you agreed to go out with me tonight. I thought I had blown it as far as you were concerned. You had every right to turn me down after the way I acted . . . the other time."

He thought *he* had blown it? She could hardly believe it.

"We could forget all about that time and call this a new start."

"No. I don't think that'll work. I like you, Vonnie, and I'd like to get things straight between us."

"Maybe I'm the one who should apologize." She looked directly into his eyes. Why were apologies so hard? "I shouldn't have touched on a subject that I knew was bound to be painful for you."

"I asked. Remember? I asked what you girls had been talking about. Your answer surprised me so, disappointed me so that I just . . ."

"*Surprised* you? *Disappointed* you? I'm sorry, but I guess I just don't understand, Pete."

"You surprised me because I didn't know you knew about Gabrielle. I should have guessed."

"It was almost the first thing Allison told me."

"That figures."

She wished she could drop the conversation right there, but she couldn't. "I can understand why you were surprised and maybe hurt at what I said, but disappointed? I don't get that at all."

"Vonnie, I liked you from the first time I saw you—that day in the hardware store when you were with your dad buying sandpaper. Then when you seemed friendly at school and . . . I thought you liked me."

"But Pete! I did like you." She closed her eyes for a moment. She had never been this open in a conversation with a boy before. She hoped Pete wouldn't think she was being too forward, coming on too strong. "It almost seemed as if there were something special between us. I mean . . . I mean . . ."

"I know. I felt it too. And that's why I was so disappointed to find out you knew about Gabrielle."

"But why? Why? Why was that so important?"

Pete squirmed and eased away from her on the couch. He watched the TV for a moment and she thought he might change the subject completely and leave her as mystified as ever. Then he looked back at her.

"Vonnie, in the past few months I've been offered more sympathy than I can handle. It's nice to know people care about you—up to a point. Pretty soon you don't know who really likes you and who just feels sorry for you. I don't want pity."

She began to understand. Hadn't Hannah told her that every girl in school had been giving Pete the eye? Unless a guy was very conceited and stuck on himself he would wonder which girls were really feeling sorry for him and which ones might really like him.

"When I met you I couldn't help being pleased that you knew nothing of my past. I guess I was hunting for a girl who liked me just because I was Pete Karmer and for no other reason. I thought you were that girl until you mentioned Gabrielle, until you offered me sympathy. And then I wasn't sure. I didn't know. And I was disappointed."

Again she was careful with her word choice. "I do like you just because you're Pete Karmer. I hope you'll believe that. I liked you that first day I saw you before I knew anything about you—before I even knew your name."

"That means a lot to me, Vonnie. I'm glad you told me. I like a girl who's totally honest with a guy."

Totally honest. Suddenly she felt very guilty about her secret.

"Guess I'd better be going," Pete said as he rose from the couch. "Thanks for inviting me in. I feel better about a lot of things now."

"Me too." Vonnie followed him to the door and snapped on the porch light. Pete reached to snap the light off again, then he took her in his arms and kissed her slowly and tenderly. He kissed her the way she had imagined he would kiss her and she was reluctant to see the kiss and their evening end. She felt as if she had been looking through a kaleidoscope, watching their relationship fall into a different and more pleasing pattern.

"Thanks for a nice evening, Vonnie. I'll see you around."

And he was gone before she could tell him she had enjoyed the evening too, before she could say a word. But now there was a good feeling between them. She felt a warmth glowing deep inside her as she watched Pete get into his car and drive off into the moonlit night.

12

Vonnie thought Pete might call her on Sunday, but he didn't. On Monday morning she went to school early to work on the jazz posters and she didn't see him until English class. He smiled and spoke and took his chair much as usual. Had she imagined that something special between them on Saturday night? She couldn't believe that she had. Then, when the bell rang, Pete was at her side walking with her to her next class before he hurried on to his own. At noon she went home for lunch, but as she walked back to school she saw Pete coming to meet her to walk the rest of the way with her. The next day she made a compromise with her mother. She ate at school every other day.

The following Sunday afternoon after Hannah was finished at the hospital she picked Vonnie up and they drove to the Ward Parkway mall to look at some fabric specials. Traffic flowed on all four lanes of the highway. Car horns honked. A boy was flying a red kite from the back seat of a blue convertible. Many people were out for a drive, celebrating the first summer-like day of spring.

"You and Pete really have become an item,"

Hannah said as they drove along. "Chad says Pete acts like a different person."

"Who does he act like?" Vonnie giggled.

"You know what I mean. He acts happier. He acts as if he enjoys going to school. And he smiles a lot. For a while he just dragged himself to classes and he hardly spoke to anyone. You're good for him, Vonnie."

And he's been good for me, she thought. "Has Chad said anything to you about going out after the jazz concert?"

"No. In fact he hasn't even invited me to the concert yet. It's not for two weeks yet. Has Pete asked you to go somewhere?"

"He said something about a triple date—you and Chad, Allison and Jeff."

"That should put the end to a perfect day."

"Well, if you don't want to . . ."

"Oh, I didn't say I didn't want to. It's just that Allison will . . . well, you know how Allison gets when she's around Jeff and Pete at the same time. We can do without that kind of aggravation."

"Maybe it'll be different this time." She shared Hannah's feelings but she hated to admit it. It would be like admitting she was afraid of Allison or at least afraid of the competition Allison offered.

"It won't be different," Hannah said. "Allison's a brat and she's not going to change. Of course, maybe she and Jeff have had more of an understanding. I'll go, of course, if Chad asks me, that is."

Hannah parked the car in the crowded parking lot and they strolled to the fabric shop. Vonnie inhaled deeply, liking the clean, new smell of the bolts of spring cottons and polyesters. Pastels. Polka dots.

Stripes. She didn't sew, but she had promised Hannah to help her choose a blouse pattern and some fabric.

"I want a jiffy pattern," Hannah said. "Quick and easy."

They perched on high stools and thumbed through the Simplicity and McCall's pattern books. "Here's a cute one." Vonnie pointed to a frilly off-the-shoulder style."

"Too many ruffles. I'm the tailored type." Hannah turned three more pages. "What do you think of this one?" She pointed to a short-sleeved, V-neck style. "I could wear it belted or unbelted and with that V-neck I could wear it over a lot of my other shirts."

"I like it," Vonnie said. "And there are just four pattern pieces. It doesn't look too hard."

Hannah wrote down the pattern number, then she chose a crisp cotton with a windowpane check in rust on white that complemented her hair. The clerk found the pattern for her, measured and cut the fabric. "That'll be six dollars, please."

Hannah paid and they left the shop. "Shall we stop for a Coke before we go home?"

"Okay."

They window-shopped as they strolled to the lunch counter in the Woolco Store. Vonnie ordered iced tea and when it arrived Hannah watched as she squeezed lemon into it.

"You really like that stuff?"

"Sure." It was the truth. She did like it. She had almost forgotten what a Coke tasted like.

"How are you coming along with the jazz posters?" Hannah asked as they sipped their drinks.

"Great. I went in early every day last week. Miss

Bell and I appointed a committee to help and we're finished with them. The jazz band committee will put them up tomorrow."

They were just finishing their drinks when Vonnie saw Pete. His back was to them and at first she thought she might be mistaken. She hoped she might be mistaken because he was with another girl. A stranger. Tall. Willowy. Dark-haired. They were looking at each other and laughing. He turned slightly and she saw for sure that it was Pete. Hannah looked where she was looking, frowned and quickly glanced back at Vonnie.

"Who's that he's with?"

Vonnie tried not to seem too crushed or too surprised but it took a lot of acting and she guessed Hannah wasn't fooled. "I don't know. I've never seen her before. She's really pretty, isn't she?" She turned slightly so Pete wouldn't see her face if he turned around.

"I've got a notion to walk right over and say hello." Hannah scowled her indignation. "Of all the . . ."

"Hannah, please! That would just embarrass . . . everyone." Vonnie felt as if there was nothing inside her but space and that she might float off like a balloon if she didn't hang onto the edge of her chair. Seeing Pete with another girl explained a lot of things. She had always wondered why he never called her on Sunday. This must be his Sunday girlfriend who lived somewhere in the city. Hannah would have known her had she lived in Roe Village.

"I just can't believe that," Hannah said as Pete and the girl walked on toward the mall exit. "Who could she *be*? I just don't understand. Pete's always been so fair and square about everything."

She tried to hide her hurt and disappointment with brave words. "Oh, come on, Hannah. Where's it written that Pete can't have another girlfriend? He's never asked me to go steady."

"But you *have* been going steady." Hannah finished her Coke with an angry sucking slurp on her straw. "Everyone at school just takes it for granted."

"I guess they shouldn't, should they? That girl looked right at home at Pete's side."

"Are you going to tell him you saw them together?"

"I don't know. I really don't know." How could she decide what she was going to do when she was in shock!

Hannah drove them home and the afternoon that had seemed so invitingly warm and sunny now seemed hot and garish, and Vonnie wished she had never agreed to go shopping with Hannah in the first place. Was she going to tell Pete she had seen him with another girl? The question bothered her the rest of the day and that night she even slept poorly, waking several times with a strange unsettled feeling . . . and then she would remember. But in the morning she began to think more clearly. She and Pete really weren't going steady. To mention seeing him yesterday would only make her appear jealous and possessive. If Pete wanted to tell her about this other girl he would, and if not, she wouldn't pry.

It was raining and the gray day matched her gray mood. She half expected Pete to avoid her, but he was as attentive as usual, and nothing that happened during the whole week gave any outward indication there was another girl in his life. She tried to forget the tall dark-haired stranger whose eyes had met

Pete's on a level, whose relaxed manner told the world she had known Pete forever.

The rain lasted all week. Sometimes it fell softly and gently, but on Friday there was thunder and lightning along with power outages and hail. She didn't mind the weather as long as there were no storm clouds in her relationship with Pete. On Friday afternoon Pete asked her for a Saturday night date. She accepted. She tried not to wonder where he might be taking that other girl on Sunday.

They went to the late movie at the mall, joining Hannah and Chad after they got there. Vonnie was glad Allison and Jeff weren't present, but she didn't say so. The movie was a science fiction film and although the boys seemed to like it, she was glad when it ended.

"I've got an idea," Pete said as they left the theater.

Chad slapped him on the back. "Treat it kindly. It's in a strange place."

Pete ignored the banter. "Look at that moon."

"Very nice moon," Hannah agreed. "Did you order it special?"

"No. I only special-order full moons and that's exactly what we're going to have in about a week. I think we should take advantage of it."

"How?" Chad asked.

"How about having a moonlight picnic after the jazz concert?" Pete asked. "The first picnic of the season! Dad wouldn't care."

"What's your dad got to do with it?" Vonnie asked. "Is he coming along?"

"You guys are really funny tonight, aren't you?"

Pete grinned at her good-naturedly. "I meant that Dad wouldn't care if we had a picnic at our place. There's a small lake and we've got a boat. We could build a bonfire, roast wieners and marshmallows, take a boat ride."

"Sounds like fun," Hannah said.

"But is there any water in the lake?" Chad asked. "We've had such a dry winter it may have evaporated or something. This past week's the first time we've had any kind of moisture in months and it wasn't enough to fill a lake."

"Let's go take a look," Pete suggested. "Come on. Get in my car. We can drive out there in just a few minutes."

"Okay," Chad said. "Let's go."

"How far is it?" Vonnie asked, looking at her watch and thinking about her midnight curfew. "It's already past eleven."

"It's not far," Pete said. "It'll just take a few minutes. And Chad's right. The lake may be very low. It wouldn't be much fun to have a lakeside picnic if there isn't any lake."

They all piled into Pete's car and he headed toward the highway. Happy Joe's. Country Kitchen. McDonald's. They passed all the fast food chains, then Pete drove a mile or so into the country before he turned onto a rough graveled road. Vonnie held onto the seat to steady herself.

"Hey!" Chad called out. "This isn't the road to your place, is it?"

"I'm taking a shortcut," Pete said. "The lake's quite a ways from the house and this road approaches it from a back acreage."

"What a road!" Hannah exclaimed as they heard

135

mud thunking against the underside of the fenders. "You're not going to get us stuck out here, are you, Pete? I mean these ruts and all that rain. . . ."

Vonnie listened to the car tires squishing through the mud and she continued to hold onto the seat as they jolted along.

"Pete, I'm afraid. . . ." The car lurched to one side, then it seemed to sink about six inches before it came to a stop.

Pete wrenched at the steering wheel as he stepped on the accelerator. Vonnie heard the tires whine and spin, but the car didn't move forward.

"Oh, man!" Chad exclaimed. "We're really into it now. No sense in spinning your wheels, Pete. You need a tow truck."

"And a tow truck would need a tow truck," Hannah said. "What are we going to *do?*"

Pete groaned. "Vonnie, maybe if you get behind the wheel you can steer while Chad and I get out and push."

"I got on my new Adidas, man," Chad said.

"So kick them off," Pete said. "I'll take my shoes off too. We can roll up our pant legs and see if we can push us loose."

"Not Chad," Hannah said. "His heart, you know. Let Chad steer and the rest of us will push."

Vonnie waited for Chad's angry reaction, but his words surprised her.

"Guess there are a few advantages to being puny. Let me get behind the wheel, Pete."

Vonnie kicked off her shoes, preparing to get out and push. She admired Chad for being able to make jokes about his heart condition. Why couldn't she do that? But it was easier for Chad, she reasoned.

Everyone had known him for years. Everyone had accepted him as he was. They were so used to him that they forgot he was different just as Pete had done a moment ago.

"Which way shall I steer?" Chad asked. "There's mud everywhere I look."

"Steer to the right," Pete said. "Maybe that shoulder is firm enough to . . ."

Vonnie felt cold mud squish between her toes as she stepped from the car and walked to a rear fender.

"I'll count to three," Pete said. "When I say go, you gun the motor, Chad, and the rest of us will push. One. Two. Three."

Chad stepped on the accelerator and Vonnie pushed, feeling the car strain forward . . . then settle back.

"Again," Pete shouted. And again he counted off. And again the wheels whined, mud flew and the car remained bogged.

"It's not going to work," Hannah said. "What a mess!"

Vonnie began wiping her feet in the coarse scratchy grass at the side of the road, hating the sticky feel of the mud.

"What are we going to do?" Hannah asked. "And what time is it? My folks will flip if I'm late and if I don't call them."

"Mine too," Vonnie said. "But I don't see a phone booth."

"Pete and I could walk back to the highway," Chad said. "We could hitch a ride into town and get my car. Maybe I could pull you out, Pete. I think there's a chain in my trunk."

"And what do you think is going to keep your car from getting stuck?" Pete asked. "That won't work."

"Okay, bright boy." Chad shrugged. "What's your thought on the matter?"

"We'll walk across this field to my house." Pete sighed. "We've got a tractor. I can tell it's going to take a tractor to haul us out of here. Dad will help. He'll gripe a lot, but he'll help. What a dummy! I should have known better. I just didn't realize we'd had this much rain this week."

"We'll go with you," Vonnie said.

"No use in that," Pete said. "You girls wait here. Get in. Lock the doors. You'll be okay. Chad and I won't be gone long."

"Pete, could you call my folks from your house?" Vonnie asked.

"And mine too?" Hannah asked.

"Okay, I'll call both your folks and we'll be back as quick as we can."

"It's scary out here," Hannah said after the boys were gone. "Maybe Chad should have stayed with us."

"We'll be okay. I just hope they get our folks called."

"Yeah, me too. I don't want to be canned for a week."

"Or forever," Vonnie said. Then suddenly it seemed as if they could think of nothing to say. Moonlight silvered the rutted road. An owl screeched in the distance and the sound raised goosebumps on Vonnie's arms. The dank, moldly smell of the mud seeped right into the car with them in spite of the closed windows.

"What time is it?" Hannah asked. "I didn't wear my watch."

Vonnie held her wrist toward the window and let the moonlight fall on her watch. "It's eleven-thirty. I wish we'd gone to the early show now."

"Yeah. We'll never make it in by midnight. I just hope Pete and Chad make those phone calls."

It was after midnight when the boys returned, riding on the fenders of the yellow and green tractor Mr. Karmer was driving. Vonnie could tell Pete had had to get his dad out of bed. His hair was tousled and he had thrown gray and black striped overalls on over a tan pajama top. Even so, Mr. Karmer took time to come over to the car window, introduce himself, and try to make them feel at ease. Then he turned to Pete.

"You get in and steer, Pete, and we'll have you out of here in no time."

Chad joined Hannah in the back seat and Pete eased behind the wheel, turning the key in the ignition.

"Did you call our folks?" Hannah asked.

Pete scowled and shook his head. "I'm really sorry, but we couldn't. The phone was out. Guess all that lightning this morning got it. But Dad'll have us out of here in just a few minutes and then it won't take long to get back to town."

Vonnie felt as if her heart had dropped to her big toe. A few minutes. Her folks would be in a panic if she was late. She and Pete had always come in before the curfew. It had happened so many times, her folks were beginning to expect it. And now this!

"It's okay, Pete," Hannah said. "When my folks hear what happened and when they know your dad was helping us and trying to get us home, they'll understand."

"I hope so."

The car jerked forward a few inches as the tractor pulled the heavy chain joining the two vehicles taut. Mud flew from beneath the tractor wheels, pinging against the car windshield. The tractor motor roared. The car lurched . . . settled back . . . strained forward again and they were free.

"Whew!" Hannah breathed a sigh. "But now what? How are we going to get back to the highway?"

"Dad will tow us to a blacktop about half a mile on down this road," Pete said.

"Some shortcuts *you* know, man," Chad said. "Next time let's take the long way, okay?"

"I won't argue with that," Pete said.

After they reached the blacktop and Mr. Karmer left them, Pete drove Chad and Hannah back to Chad's car, then he drove Vonnie home.

"Good grief!" Vonnie exclaimed as she grabbed her shoes and headed for the front door. "I think every light in the house is on. What a welcome!"

"I'm sorry, Vonnie. Let me do the talking. I'll try to explain to them."

Both her parents were standing in the hallway when they opened the door and before she or Pete could speak, they both started talking at once.

"Do you realize what time it is?" Her father glared at her, shouted at her.

"Where have you *been?*" her mother demanded.

"Young man," her father said, glaring at Pete. "Vonnie was supposed to be home over an hour ago."

"We had problems, Mr. Morrison," Pete began. "I . . ."

"I don't want to hear your excuses." The words dismissed Pete, and her father was glaring at her again, his mouth set in a grim thinness.

"It wasn't Pete's fault," Vonnie said. "We . . ."

"I'm sorry, Vonnie," Pete said.

She saw Pete glaring back at her parents. For a moment his chin thrust upward and forward like a chunk of granite. Then he turned and left, not bothering to close the door behind him. Vonnie rushed onto the porch, intending to call after him. But what could she say? She was defeated, defeated by her parents as well as by Pete. For a moment she stood there in the cold glare of the porch light, then she turned and went back inside.

"How could you!" She glared from her father to her mother and back again. "How could you talk to us like that! How could you refuse to listen to Pete! How could you be so unfair!"

"How could *you* be so unfair?" her father demanded. "Surely you knew we would be frantic when you weren't home on time. Surely you could have had the courtesy to telephone us."

"I tried."

"You must not have tried very hard. We've been here all evening," her father said.

Then her mother took a deep breath and Vonnie saw her fists unclench as she wiped her hands on her slacks. "Maybe we all better simmer down and talk this over in the morning."

"I think you should hear my side of it right now," Vonnie insisted. "I'll make it short. We were with Hannah and Chad. Pete drove us into the country to look over a place for a picnic. We got stuck in mud and had to get his dad to tow us out with his tractor. Pete tried to call you, but the storms had left their phone out of order. That's the story."

"And we sat here wondering where you were," her father said. "Wondering if you had passed out. Wondering if anyone at all would know what to do for you if you had. We called hospitals. We called the police. We . . ."

"Enough," her mother said. "She's home. She's well. She's safe. We won't discuss it any more until the morning."

"How will I ever face Pete again?" Vonnie asked. "Had you thought of that? Had you thought at all about *his* feelings?"

13

Your mother's right, Vonnie." Her father raked his fingers through his hair. The grim tightness of his mouth softened a bit. "Let's go to bed now. Time enough to discuss this tomorrow when we've all cooled down."

"I'm sorry I caused you so much worry." She was sorry for that. In spite of her anger at her parents' unfairness she felt guilty about the fear and worry she had put them through. At the time they had had no way of knowing it couldn't be helped. But now that they knew . . .

"We know you didn't intend to give us a scare," her mother said. "I appreciate the fact that you tried to call us. But it's the end result of your actions that we're going to have to reach an agreement about. Tomorrow. A good night's sleep will work wonders for everyone."

Her mother stepped to her side and gave her a hug, but Vonnie still felt such a hot tightness inside herself that she could barely offer a thin smile in return. Tomorrow wasn't going to change the basic situation. The bottom line was the same.

Vonnie went upstairs first, hurriedly prepared for bed, snapped off her light. Then she lay staring at the ceiling, barely conscious of the moonlight that was shafting through her window and washing her room in a milky paleness. She was relieved that her parents had cooled down. She couldn't recall ever having seen her father so angry. And the memory of the stark fear she had seen in her mother's eyes filled her with guilt. They would talk about their differences the next day. She might not like the conclusions they would reach or the decisions they would make, but there would be understanding between them. Basically, her parents were fair-minded.

But what about Pete? When she thought of how he must be feeling hot tears stung her eyes. She remembered the angry jut of his chin as he had left the house. If he had stayed a little longer maybe her parents would have apologized. Pete deserved an apology. He had been a guest, her guest, and her parents had treated him almost as if he didn't exist, didn't matter. Except for yelling at him once, her father had acted as if Pete weren't even there.

Maybe she could call him tomorrow. No. His phone was out. She sniffed and buried her head in her pillow. The phone line wasn't the only reason she couldn't call him. There was that other girl. She felt almost sure that Pete had some sort of a standing date with that girl on Sundays.

Yet that was silly. She had nothing to back up such an assumption—just the fact that she had seen them together once and the fact that he never called her on Sunday. She tried not to cry, but she felt a tear trickle down her cheek. Tonight's bummer would probably send Pete to that other girl on a full time basis. And she really couldn't blame him for his feelings.

The next morning she dressed in her most comfortable jeans and sweater, hoping that comfort on the outside would ease the discomfort on the inside. She delayed going downstairs for as long as she could, but when she reached the kitchen her parents were still at the table lingering over coffee and reading the headlines in *The Times*. Her dad was in work khakis and a black sweat shirt, but her mother had on the green pantsuit she wore when she was going out to do errands.

"Good morning, Vonnie," her mother said.

Her father smiled at her, but his smile was like the thick layer of frosting she sometimes put on a near-failure cake to cover up the problem underneath.

"Good morning." She sighed. "But let's not pretend everything's okay. I feel miserable about last night."

"It wasn't as bad as all that, I suppose," her father said.

"There's no problem we can't solve." Her mother brought her a glass of orange juice and eased the milk pitcher and an empty tumbler toward her.

"I guess not." Vonnie sipped the tangy juice. "But I don't know how I'm ever going to face Pete again."

"I'll face him with an apology if you'll face him with the truth," her father said. "I spoke thoughtlessly and I'm sorry."

Vonnie heard her cue. Her father was trying to make it easy for her to give in. She knew it wouldn't be easy for him to apologize to Pete. Apologies were never easy. But it wasn't easy for her to give in either.

"How about it, Vonnie?" her mother asked. "Don't you think you're well enough acquainted at school, well enough acquainted with Pete to give up being so secretive about . . ."

Vonnie stared at her milk glass and although she hated admitting it to herself she knew the whole big deal last night was not her parents' fault nor was it Pete's fault. It was her own fault for withholding information that could have made everyone feel more at ease.

"I suppose I'm just making things harder for you."

"Harder for everyone," her father said. "If I'd felt that Pete knew what to do to help you in an emergency I wouldn't have been so worked up when you were late."

"And Pete would have understood why we were so uptight," her mother said.

"All right." Vonnie gulped the rest of her milk. "If Pete's still speaking to me tomorrow I'll tell him the truth, the whole truth and nothing but the truth." She tried to make light of her decision, but she knew she had failed.

"If he's still speaking to you?" her father asked. "Surely he's not going to cut you out of his life over a misunderstanding until he's heard your explanation."

"You could telephone him," her mother said. "It might be easier for you if you paved the way for a face-to-face meeting with a phone call."

As she thought of Pete's Sunday girlfriend she could feel heat rising to her face and she knew she was blushing. "I can't call him, Mom. His phone's out, remember?"

"Maybe it's fixed by now."

"I doubt if the telephone linemen work on Sunday," her father said.

She smiled weakly at her father. She wasn't about to tell her parents about the other girl she had seen with Pete. "I'll just have to talk to Pete tomorrow at school, but it won't be easy."

Somehow Sunday dragged by. She called Hannah about mid-afternoon to see how she had fared with her parents.

"I lucked out, Vonnie. Can you believe it! They had gone out to some friends for the evening and I got home before they did."

"Did you tell them what happened to us?"

"Yeah, I told them about getting stuck and about Pete's dad having to tow us with the tractor. They didn't even ask what time it all happened, so I didn't tell them."

"No use asking for problems."

"What happened with you and your folks?"

"Plenty. They were right up the wall. Dad yelled at Pete and Pete left angry. And tomorrow I'll have to talk to him—to apologize."

"I'm really sorry, Vonnie. Maybe I can help."

"I don't see how. It's just between Pete and me."

"I suppose you're right. But if I can put in a good word for you, I will. You can depend on that."

"Thanks, Hannah. You're a pal."

After Vonnie hung up she talked to her parents again. "I'm just going to tell Pete my secret. Nobody else."

"Was that Hannah you were talking to on the phone?" her dad asked.

"Yes."

"You're not going to tell her?"

"No." Vonnie heard her voice go shrill as it always did when she was tense about something. "I'm only going to tell Pete and I'm going to swear him to secrecy—if he'll listen to me."

She was relieved that her parents didn't push her

any farther. And she was relieved that her mother hadn't reminded her yet again about Joanie Hanson back in Washington. Everyone in school had known about Joanie's epilepsy, yet she had been elected prom queen. Well, Vonnie knew she wasn't the prom queen type. She was just plain old Vonnie Morrison and she needed privacy in personal matters.

On Monday she walked to school with Hannah and although facing Pete and talking with him was uppermost in her mind, she and Hannah discussed other things. The new Spanish workbook. The oral book report for English. The picnic Pete had mentioned having, following the jazz concert.

"I don't know if I'm still invited or not," Vonnie said.

"Listen, Vonnie, maybe it would help you if you tried to think about Saturday night from Pete's point of view."

"I have been. He's probably furious. He's probably going to cut me dead the first time we meet face to face."

"Oh come on! Pete's probably really feeling guilty about the whole thing. It was a dum-dum stunt to try to take that shortcut after all that rain. And it was his idea to go to the lake when he knew we both had a midnight curfew."

"Maybe so, but . . ."

"No buts, Vonnie. Pete's probably really been kicking himself over what happened. He probably spent all day yesterday wondering if you're mad at him, wondering if your dad has forbidden you to go out with him again. Guys worry too, you know."

"Yeah. He was probably chewing his nails all the

time he was taking his Sunday girlfriend out for the afternoon—and maybe the evening too."

Hannah said no more as they approached the schoolhouse and Vonnie felt very much alone. How could the sunlight be slanting onto the weathered brick the same way it always did? How could all the kids be standing around in little cliques as they always did? Didn't the sun and the bricks and the kids know that nothing was the same as it had been two days ago!

She hadn't expected to see Pete before school. Instead of rehearsing only a few mornings a week, the jazz band had been meeting every morning in order to prepare for the concert and clinic. And Mr. Claribone kept them until the last minute before the bell rang, barely giving them time to put the instruments in their cases and get to their next class on time. Pete came into the English room only seconds before the late bell rang. He brushed by Vonnie's chair without looking directly at her and she wouldn't allow herself to turn and look at him. All through the endless book reports she wondered if he was staring at the back of her head.

After class Pete didn't hurry to catch up with her and it wasn't until noon that she saw him again. She was relieved when he spoke first. Her tongue felt like a paste dauber and she doubted if she could make it work.

"Vonnie, I want to talk with you."

His direct approach surprised her. Was he going to break off with her completely? He was so serious and unsmiling she swallowed and forced herself to answer. "I want to talk with you too, Pete."

"I'm glad." Now he fell in step beside her. "I

thought, well, I was afraid . . . maybe you wouldn't be speaking to me."

"I have something to tell you, Pete."

"Then let's get our lunch and find a table to ourselves."

She welcomed the rush of voices that masked the thudding of her heart and the pleasant fragrance of oregano had a calming effect. But she wasn't hungry. She chose soup, milk, an apple, and she noticed that Pete wasn't eating his usual heavy lunch. He had chosen a ham salad sandwich and only one carton of milk. No full meal. No dessert.

"Let's sit at the far end of that table where the freshmen usually eat," Pete suggested. "None of our crowd will bother us there."

She headed for the table, trying to plan what she would say to Pete. She couldn't just blurt out the truth. She would have to ease into it, approach it in a way that wouldn't make her look too far-out and freaky. But once they sat down Pete began talking and she made no attempt to interrupt.

"I've been thinking about Saturday night all weekend, Vonnie. Yesterday was really . . . hell. I wanted to call you so badly, but the phone was still out. That's the way it is with rural lines—it takes a while to get repairs."

You could have driven to another phone, she thought. She opened her carton of milk.

"I suppose I could have driven to another phone," he said as if reading her mind, "but I wasn't sure you'd even speak to me. I wasn't sure your folks would *let* you speak to me."

"Pete, I'm really sorry about Saturday night. It wasn't your fault, and . . ."

"Listen to me, Vonnie. It *was* my fault. And I

want to apologize—to you and to your parents. I shouldn't have insisted on going out to the lake when it already was so late. I don't blame your folks for being so upset. They don't know me all that well and . . . well, I can understand their concern. But it's you—us I'm really worried about. Is everything okay between us, Vonnie?"

She smiled up at him as relief and happiness flooded through her. "Of course everything's okay, Pete." She knew then that she wasn't going to tell him her secret. Not yet. What good purpose would it serve? Pete was apologizing to her! She didn't have to tell all. "Everyone really went bonkers Saturday night, Pete, but my folks had calmed down a lot by yesterday. Dad wants to apologize to you. He told me so. Pete, could we just pretend Saturday night didn't happen? Let's just blot it out of our minds and forget all about it."

Pete grinned down at her. "You're really okay, Vonnie. I know you must have caught a lot of flak from your folks. I caught a little from mine too. If you're willing to forgive and forget, so am I."

He took her hand and suddenly the whole world seemed warm and bright again. Pete wasn't angry at her. She wasn't angry at him. And she still had her secret.

14

The all-is-well feeling that Vonnie had enjoyed all day at school faded quickly as she and Hannah began to walk home that afternoon. She hadn't done what she had promised her parents she would do and she knew her mother would ask her about it first thing after she stepped through the doorway. How was she going to handle the questions? She considered inviting Hannah in, but she rejected the idea. It wasn't fair to use a friend as a delaying tactic.

"That you, Vonnie?" her mother called from the third floor as Vonnie closed the front door.

"Right, Mom." She ran upstairs to her room. She usually hurried right to the attic, if her mother was up there, to see what her project of the day had been. But today she went to her room and changed from her school outfit to old jeans and a sweat shirt. In a matter of moments her mother stopped at her doorway to talk with her.

"How did it go with Pete?"

She sighed. Her mother was never one to beat around the bush about things. "Everything's fine." She put on a bright smile. "We had a long talk at lunch and Pete was very understanding . . . about *everything.*" She felt guilty. She had never lied to her mother before. And she hadn't lied to her now, had she? Everything *was* fine between her and Pete, and Pete had been very understanding about everything . . . about everything that they had discussed, that is. She couldn't help it if her mother drew the wrong conclusions, could she?

"I'm so glad, Vonnie." Her mother hugged her and she felt her throat tighten at her deception. Or maybe it was just the smell of turpentine clinging to her mother's green smock that made her nose and throat feel so strange.

"I can remember how it feels to be on the outs with someone you care very much about," her mother said. "I was seventeen once too."

Vonnie looked at her mother trying to imagine how she must have looked at seventeen. She couldn't. Her mother was her mother. She had probably been old even when she was seventeen.

"Pete said he would apologize to both you and Dad for stomping off the way he did."

Her mother laughed a bit ruefully. "I guess apologies are due from us too. Why don't you ask Pete to dinner some evening?"

"Oh, Mom. That would be so formal . . . and sort of scary . . . for him, I mean. He's coming over Wednesday night to study with me for a Spanish test. Couldn't you and Dad just talk to him then? I mean, keep it casual, like no big deal?"

"Maybe that would be best." Her mother went on downstairs and Vonnie felt as if she had just cleared a high hurdle.

That night at the dinner table she and her dad skirted the same subject she and her mother had skirted that afternoon and again she did not lie. Not really. If her father wanted to jump to his own conclusions, that wasn't her fault . . . was it? She had read somewhere that people hear what they want to hear. That's what her parents had done. They hadn't heard what she actually had said, they had heard what they wanted to hear. But if that was true, why did she feel so rotten about it?

On Wednesday night the atmosphere grew stiff and formal as Pete greeted her parents. She guessed that he had been rehearsing his lines all day, probably for several days. He had dressed up a little more than usual—brown cords and his best tan V-neck over his favorite brown and white gingham shirt.

"I'm sorry for bringing Vonnie in so late last Saturday, Mr. and Mrs. Morrison. I know Vonnie has told you the reason, but I want you to know it won't happen again."

"I'm sure it won't, Pete," her father said. "We were all upset that night. I'm sorry I raised my voice, lost control."

"And that's that," Vonnie said. "No more apologies. No more looking back, okay?"

"Okay." Pete said, and her father nodded his agreement.

"You two make yourselves at home," her mother said. "I have some things to take care of upstairs and your dad's going to be working in the basement." Her parents left them alone and Vonnie appreciated their giving her and Pete the privacy of the living room.

"That wasn't so bad," Pete said, smiling at her as they sat down on the couch and opened their workbooks on the coffee table.

"Not so bad, but I'm glad it's over and I know you are too." And she knew she was going to have to tell

Pete about her diabetes. Soon. She couldn't live with the half-lies that were crammed like a wedge between herself and her parents. But not tonight. She wouldn't tell him tonight and risk spoiling the new warmth of feeling that she could feel growing between them.

They worked on Spanish verbs for half an hour or so, then they changed pace and drilled on vocabulary. When they finished, Vonnie went to the kitchen and opened a diet Pepsi for herself and a Coke for Pete.

Pete had cleared their books from the coffee table by the time she returned with the drinks and she set their glasses in the silver coasters her mother always kept there. The apologies were past. The studying was finished. Now they could really relax. Pete was hunched slightly forward, elbows on knees, but when she sat down beside him he leaned back, put his arm around her and drew her close.

"Vonnie, there's something very special about you—something very special between us."

She looked up at him without speaking, and he bent to kiss her, a tender but quick kiss that told her he had something else to say. She smiled, ready to listen. For a moment Pete fumbled for something in his pocket, then he pulled out a small wad of crumpled tissue paper. He unfolded the paper carefully until he reached a small shiny object which he placed on the palm of his hand. He held it toward her.

"Pete! A tiny trumpet. It's really neat." She picked it up and admired it. A pin. About an inch long. Its brassy finish gleamed in the lamplight. "Where did you get it?"

"Mr. Claribone gave everyone in jazz band a pin representing his instrument. It's engraved on the back with my initials and the year."

"That makes it very special." She turned the pin over to read the engraving, then gave it back to Pete. "Aren't you going to wear it? How come you don't have it pinned on your sweater?"

"I'd like for you to wear it, Vonnie." Pete's direct gaze bored into hers. "If you'd wear it, it would mean we were sort of . . . well, it would mean we were going steady."

She was so surprised she blurted out the first thing that flashed into her mind. "But what about . . ."

"Gabrielle? Vonnie, I thought you knew by now that I'm not carrying a torch for Gabrielle. She was an important part of my past, true. But what's past is past. I've been looking to the future for some time now."

Vonnie felt as if a perfect evening had suddenly come apart like a jigsaw puzzle jostled by a careless hand.

"I wasn't thinking of Gabrielle . . . not exactly." She squirmed and looked away, hating to refuse Pete's pin, yet unable to accept it without a better understanding between them.

"Then what are you thinking of? I thought you liked me. I thought we had a very special thing going between us. Do your parents object to your going steady, is that it?"

"I don't think they'd really object. It's just that . . ."

"Just that you don't really like me all that much, is that it? Is there someone else you want to go out with?"

"There's nobody else *I* want to go out with. But what about *you?*"

"What *about* me?" Pete looked at her with genuine puzzlement written on his face. She wanted to believe that everything was honest and aboveboard between them, yet she thought of her parents. People hear what they want to hear. People believe what they want to believe. She wanted to believe that Pete really wanted to go steady with her, yet she didn't want to fool herself. That would only lead to pain later.

"What about me, Vonnie?" Pete asked again. "Have I done something, said something?" He laid the pin on the coffee table.

She cleared her throat and forced herself to speak out. "I saw you with that other girl. I mean it's okay and everything if you want to go out with her, but it's not fair for you to try to make me think we're going steady. Or maybe you've broken up with her? Is that it?" She hoped those last questions didn't make her sound too eager. Had Pete heard the wistfulness in her voice? She hoped not.

"What other girl are you talking about?"

Vonnie felt as if a hand were squeezing her voice box. She could hardly speak. It wasn't fair for Pete to make her have to spell it out for him. But she would. Better now than later.

"I'm talking about a dark-haired girl. A girl almost as tall as you are. A very pretty girl. Hannah and I saw you with her one Sunday afternoon at the Ward Parkway mall."

Now Pete was smiling. "That was Dianne. My *cousin* Dianne. She's not a girlfriend. My mom and her mom are twin sisters and she lives in Shawnee

Mission. Our family either goes to their house or they come to our house almost every Sunday. That's who you saw me with. Gosh, Vonnie, if you had let me know, if you had come over and said hello, I would have introduced you. Dianne's no big secret or anything."

She wanted to believe him. More than anything in the world she wanted to believe him. And his story made sense. Sunday was a family day for lots of people. Just because she and her parents didn't have much family didn't mean that other people didn't. And the girl . . . Dianne . . . Dianne actually looked a lot like Pete when she stopped to think about it. Same height. Same dark hair. Same blue eyes.

"What a dope I've been, Pete. I never thought about a guy going around with his cousin."

"Then you'll wear my pin?" He picked up the pin again and offered it to her.

"I'd like to wear it. I'd be *proud* to wear it." She took the tiny trumpet and pinned it to her shirt, then smiled at him. "I've never been so happy, Pete. Never."

Pete pulled her close and they kissed with such a slow sweet tenderness that Vonnie wanted it to go on forever. When they parted she leaned her head on Pete's chest for a moment, then they kissed again. And the parting was no easier the second time.

"I'd better be going now, Vonnie." Pete stood reluctantly, gathered his books, then smiled down at her. "It's really been a great evening."

"The greatest." She walked with him to the door and he kissed her quickly and gently before he left. She watched as he walked to his car and drove off.

Then she sighed. She was going steady with Pete Karmer. She could hardly believe it was true.

When she was ready for bed she pinned Pete's trumpet to her rose-sprigged pajamas and the next morning she pinned it to her blue turtleneck sweater. It was so tiny. Would anyone notice it? In one way she wanted everyone to notice it, to know she and Pete were steadies. But in another way she wanted their relationship to be a sweet secret just between the two of them.

She was surprised that neither of her parents noticed the pin at the breakfast table, but she didn't call it to their attention. Plenty of time to break the news later. Would they be pleased? They never had discussed her going steady. There had been no reason to discuss such a thing. Pete was the first boyfriend she had gone out with.

Once she left the house it was a different matter. Hannah noticed the pin first thing.

"Vonnie! Pete gave you his pin! Neat!"

What could she say? She just smiled at first. "We're going steady, Hannah. He asked me last night."

"I'm glad, Vonnie. You and Pete are really right for each other."

They got to school a bit early and before the last bell rang lots of kids had seen or heard about her pin. Some of the girls came around to look it over and others just stood at a distance, but the word traveled fast. It wasn't until she took her snack break that she learned exactly what some of the girls were thinking about her.

She had just stepped into the alcove off the restroom and had pulled the privacy curtain carefully. Nobody had been in the restroom when she entered, but a few minutes later she heard the door swish open and she recognized Hannah's voice. And Allison's. And another girl's—maybe Janie Croley's. She couldn't be really sure who the third girl was. But it didn't matter. What mattered was what the girls were saying. About her.

"When did he give it to her?" Allison asked.

"Last night," Hannah said. "Isn't that neat? I don't think Chad's about to part with his. How about Jeff?"

Allison didn't answer and the third girl spoke. "I don't see what Pete sees in *her*. I think she's stand-offish. A snob."

"She really isn't," Hannah said. "Not when you get to know her."

"Well, she sticks to herself an awful lot," the other girl said. "She acts like she's too hoity-toity to eat in the cafeteria, and when she does eat at school it's just because Pete has insisted. And I *hate* teacher's pets."

"What makes you think she's a teacher's pet?" Hannah asked. "She studies hard and works hard. She deserves what she gets."

"But she doesn't get *everything* she deserves," Allison said with mock sweetness. "She's always sneaking candy during class. I see her. You've seen her. You can't tell me the teachers don't see it happen too. But they don't do anything about it."

"Yeah," the other girl agreed. "You know how strict Chard is about school rules! If any of us got caught sneaking candy we'd get detention. I don't understand how Vonnie gets by with it. It isn't fair."

"I'd like to fix her wagon," Allison said. "And I just may."

"If you tattle on her to the teachers you'll just make yourself look bad," Hannah said.

"Who said anything about tattling?" Allison laughed sharply. "When I get even with her, she's really going to know she's had it."

"Allison!" Hannah exclaimed. "For gosh sakes!"

"Make it for *Pete's* sake," Allison said. "I'm getting tired of going out with Jeff all the time and now that Pete seems to be over his thing with Gabrielle, it shouldn't be too hard for me to get him looking my way. That would fix little Vonnie but good. You can tell her I said so for all I care."

"Making a play for Pete would be a dirty trick, Allison," Hannah said.

"All's fair in love and war. It's a cliché, but it's going to be my motto."

The other girl laughed. "Personally, I don't think you can score with Pete, Allison. After all, you've been trying for years."

"Want to put any money where your mouth is?" Allison asked.

Vonnie didn't hear the girl's reply as feet scraped against the tile and the restroom door opened and closed. She felt sick. She hadn't realized how her actions had been coming across to the rest of the girls. She could hardly believe they thought she was snobbish, yet she realized that they must. At least Hannah was different. Hannah knew her better than the others. Hannah understood her . . . didn't she? She hurried from the alcove and headed for the media center not knowing how she was going to cope. She knew Allison would be a formidable enemy. If she dropped Jeff and gave her full attention to winning Pete, she would probably succeed.

15

Vonnie wished she could stay at school for lunch that day. Did she have to go home? Her mother was expecting her, but she could call and make other arrangements. She had a dime and there was a pay phone in the gym. She made the call. And she worried the rest of the morning about the conversation she had overheard in the restroom.

"Hey, thought you were going home this noon," Hannah said to her as Vonnie joined the usual group at the lunch table nearest the window. Had Allison been scowling before she arrived? Her scowl made her eyes look very green.

"Changed my mind at the last minute," Vonnie said. *You and Allison changed my mind for me,* she thought. She felt very uneasy about the conversation she had overheard. Would Hannah tell her about Allison's threat, the other girl's dare? It would be sort of a test. If Hannah were really her friend . . . But friends didn't test each other. It was a rotten thought.

"What's the matter, Vonnie?" Pete asked.

"Nothing. Why?"

"Well then, do you want to do it?"

"Do what? What are you talking about?"

"See? You didn't hear a word we were saying. Sure you're okay?"

"I'm fine." She felt her face growing hot. "I was just thinking about something else . . . about the Spanish assignment for this afternoon."

"You do want to go on a picnic after the jazz concert, don't you?" Hannah asked.

"Sure she does." Chad gave her a teasing look. "And she knows a real neat shortcut to the lake, don't you, Vonnie?"

"Several of us know that shortcut, don't we?" She smiled. How crazy! A few days ago she didn't think she would ever look back and smile at the thought of being bogged down in that mud hole.

"Lay off, Chad," Pete said. "Next time we'll take the long way. No more shortcuts and that's a promise. How about it, Vonnie? You for the picnic?"

"Sure. Sounds like fun."

"When can we all meet to make plans?" Hannah asked.

"Why don't you all come over to my house tonight after supper?" Allison asked. "We can rap about it then."

"What time?" Jeff asked.

"How about seven-thirty?" Allison looked at Pete for confirmation rather than at Jeff and Vonnie shivered as if someone had laid a cold hand on the back of her neck.

"Seven-thirty's okay with me," Pete said. "It shouldn't take long to make a few plans. Food. Drinks. Tapes for the tape deck."

"What about the boat?" Chad asked. "We'll want to go for a boat ride, won't we?"

"A moonlight boat ride." Allison breathed the words, glancing up at Pete as she brushed her long silky hair over her shoulders. "It sounds really romantic."

Jeff gave Allison a playful shove. "You probably don't even know which end of the oar to put in the water."

"Why should I bother with learning about oars when there'll be all of you big strong guys to take care of that sort of thing for me?"

Pete eased a bit closer to Vonnie on the cafeteria bench, letting his hand touch hers and looking down at her as if he were unaware that Allison had been looking at him when she made her last remark.

"Shall we say seven-thirty at Allison's for sure?" Hannah asked.

Chad and Pete nodded, and Jeff slapped Chad on the shoulder. "How about picking me up? I've got no wheels tonight."

"It's a deal," Chad replied. "I'll stop for you first, Hannah, then we'll swing around the loop and get Jeff."

"I'll give you a ride, Vonnie," Pete said. Then he looked up at the group. "Everyone bring some ideas for food and entertainment, okay?"

Vonnie didn't have a chance to talk to Hannah until after school and then she didn't know how to approach the subject. Should she come right out and tell Hannah she had overheard everything? Or should she play dumb? Or should she just wait and see if Hannah would mention the conversation to her? She thought the decision was a big one until they left the schoolhouse, then suddenly her words came tumbling out almost like lines from a well-rehearsed play.

"Hannah, there's something I've got to tell you."

"What?" Hannah flipped her ponytail over her shoulder and glanced sharply at Vonnie. "Nothing's wrong between you and Pete, is there?"

"Why do you ask that?"

Hannah's face flushed and she looked away.

"That was unfair of me, Hannah. I'm sorry." She went on talking quickly before she could change her mind. "What I started to say, started to tell you was that I overheard the things you and Allison and that other girl said in the restroom this morning."

"But how? We were . . . alone. I thought we were alone."

"I was in the alcove. Behind the privacy curtain."

"Listening? How did you know we were coming in?"

"I wasn't *intentionally* listening, Hannah! I was just in the alcove lying down for a few minutes. I . . . wasn't feeling too good, but I didn't want to go to the nurse and have her take my temp and all that stuff. I didn't mean to listen. Really I didn't. I didn't think anyone was going to say anything important. And then when the conversation began to get . . . sticky . . . well, I was too embarrassed to let anyone know I had heard."

For a few moments Hannah was silent and Vonnie knew Hannah must be trying to remember exactly what had been said.

"I didn't know I was coming across so snobbish to the kids, Hannah. I thought it was neat of you to stick up for me."

"I know you aren't a snob, Vonnie. But I can see how others might feel that way about you. No hard feelings, but really I can understand it. If I didn't know you better, I might think that too."

"Just because I eat lunch at home?"

"That's only part of it. Most of the kids eat at school and of course going home makes you seem different, but nobody really cares where you eat your lunch. I think it's the stuff you get by with in class that really puts some of the kids down on you. Miss Chard prides herself on running a tight ship. She thinks a teacher who overlooks small infractions of the rules will be faced with larger infractions. That's why she's so strict about gum chewing or eating in the classroom."

"I never chew gum."

"You know what I mean." Hannah gave her a sidelong glance. "Don't try to tell me you never eat candy in class. I've seen you. All the kids have seen you do it. But the teachers *never* seem to see you. It's like you're Little Miss Perfect or something."

"I didn't know there were such strict rules about candy in the classroom."

"Obviously. But now you know. Why don't you do yourself a favor and knock off eating until you're out of school?"

"I will." She said the words with conviction, but she was wondering how she would live up to them. The threat of insulin shock could sneak up quickly. She supposed that whenever she felt lightheaded and shaky she could leave the room and eat a mint in the privacy of the deserted hallway. But surely leaving the room would cause more comment than sneaking the candy she needed to combat too much insulin. She could sense Hannah looking at her in puzzlement.

"I suppose you heard what Allison said about . . . about Pete." They had reached a street corner

166

and Hannah was so intent on their conversation she stumbled over the curbing.

"Of course. Gosh, Hannah, I wish I could pretend it didn't bother me, but it does. It bothers me a lot."

"Allison talks big, Vonnie. Don't let her bluff you."

"In a way she is trying to bluff me, isn't she? She said she didn't care if you told me. I think she wanted you to tell me."

"Vonnie, all the kids in jazz band are very proud of those pins Mr. Claribone awarded to his outstanding players. Just remember you're the one who's wearing Pete's pin. He didn't give it to Allison. I feel sorry for Jeff. He's the one who's going to be hurt if Allison meant what she said."

"There are a lot of girls who would like to go out with Jeff."

"Could be, but Jeff wants to go with Allison. He's going to be hurt when she goes into her act."

"Her act?"

"The act she tried the night you and Pete first joined us at That Place. Jeff's a sharp guy where most things are concerned, but when it comes to Allison his backbone turns to boiled spaghetti and his brain to mush."

"Hannah . . . I was really pleased that you stuck up for me today. I mean . . . I know how easy it would have been just to have agreed with Allison to keep the peace."

"That's not my style, Vonnie. I stick up for my opinions when I'm around Allison and you can stick up for yourself too. You know, another person really can't put you down unless you let her."

"Now you're making me sound wishy-washy."

"No way. I'm just telling you that you can hold your own with Allison if you decide to. You're good therapy for Pete. Hang in there."

"You make me sound like some sort of medication. A bitter pill maybe."

"Hey! Forget it. I'll see you tonight. I think Pete's picnic is going to be a lot of fun."

They had reached Vonnie's house and she hoped Hannah didn't notice her sigh. She wasn't all that enthusiastic about the moonlight picnic. There were a lot of things she would have to consider. She still felt guilty about letting her parents think she had told Pete about her diabetes. She honestly had planned to tell him soon, but right now would be the worst time ever. How could she! Not after Allison had declared open season on Pete. Allison Moore didn't look as if she had ever been sick a day in her entire life.

The house seemed cool and quiet after the warmth of the afternoon sunshine and the heat of her conversation with Hannah. She smelled ham and beans simmering on the stove as she entered the kitchen.

"Mom?" No reply. She made herself a snack and ate it, washing the saltiness of the Wheat Thins down with ice cold milk.

After she rinsed out her milk glass she went to her room and began doing homework. She didn't think her parents would mind her going to Allison's house for an hour or so on a school night, but just to be on the safe side she wanted to be able to tell them her homework was finished.

"Sure you can go to Allison's for a while," her

mother had said as they ate dinner. "But what about this picnic you kids are planning? Do Pete's folks know about it?"

"I'm sure they do, Mom. Pete said his dad would use the tractor to help haul firewood down to the lake shore. But I'll be able to tell you the details after tonight's meeting."

"I thought you weren't too keen for that Moore girl," her father said.

"I know. I'm not. But she's Jeff's girl and Jeff's Pete's best friend." She sighed. "There's not much I can do to avoid her."

"Well, Hannah will be along," her mother said. "I'm sure you'll have a good time."

Pete called for her a little before seven-thirty, but Jeff and Chad and Hannah were already at Allison's house when they arrived. She lived in the Bel Aire Hills development where each split level home sat on two acres of carefully manicured ground. Pete turned onto the curving horseshoe drive in front of the red brick house, parking behind Chad's car. When they stepped onto the porch she pushed the doorbell button on one side of the massive double doors and the doorbell chimed the theme from "Moon River."

In moments Mrs. Moore greeted them. She was a tiny sparrow-like woman and Vonnie thought she did look old enough to be Allison's grandmother. After Pete introduced Vonnie to her, Mrs. Moore turned toward the living room.

"Allie, baby, the rest of your little guests are here."

Allie baby? Vonnie squelched a laugh. The laugh died completely when Allison appeared.

"Hi, Pete." Allison ignored Vonnie. "We've been waiting for you. Come on in."

Pete stepped back to let Vonnie enter first and she felt her shoes press into the deep pile of an Oriental area rug that lay on the celery-colored carpeting of the foyer.

"About time you got here," Jeff called from the living room. "Let's get cracking."

Hannah waved at Vonnie from where she was sitting by Chad on the floor near the fireplace. At first Vonnie thought the fire was real. Then she noticed there was no warmth coming from the logs and that the effect of a fire was produced by a subtly hidden electric bulb.

Vonnie sat down on a brocaded couch and Pete dropped down beside her. Instead of seating herself beside Jeff, Allison sat down on the other side of Pete. Tonight she was wearing purple satin jeans that fitted like her skin and a lavender sweater that snugged over her figure. Her long golden hair was flowing loose and everything about her gave the effect of a fragile violet. A false effect, Vonnie thought with irritation.

"Allie, baby," her mother said, "I'll be in the kitchen. Let me know when you're ready for some goodies."

"I will, Mama."

For a moment Vonnie almost felt sorry for Allison. Sometimes she thought her parents were overprotective. How would she have coped with a mother like Allison's?

Once Mrs. Moore left the room Jeff spoke up again. "Let's get down to business. What are we going to have to eat on this picnic?"

"Hot dogs," Chad said. "Can't have a picnic without hot dogs."

"How about Wranglers?" Pete asked. "That's your favorite kind, isn't it, Allison?"

"Right!" Allison beamed at him. "They're the best."

"They're too fat," Hannah said. "They slip out of the bun."

"Okay." Pete pulled a notebook and pencil from his pocket. "We'll get one package of skinny hot dogs and one package of Wranglers. What else?"

"Chips," Hannah said. "Potato chips and corn curls."

"Don't forget something to drink," Allison said. "You know my favorite, Pete."

"Cream soda." Pete jotted the words onto the list. "Anyone else got a favorite?"

"Pepsi for me," Chad said.

"Me too," Jeff said.

"How about a diet Pepsi?" Vonnie asked.

"That's okay for those who like soapsuds." Allison giggled.

Vonnie ignored Allison's comment and giggle, but she noticed it. And she also noticed that Allison was sitting closer and closer to Pete. Jeff was getting a steely glint in his eyes.

"How about some deviled eggs?" Vonnie asked. "I'll make some if everyone likes them."

"Sounds great," Pete said.

"But sort of messy," Allison said.

"No messier than any of this other stuff." Hannah grinned. "And how about marshmallows? We'll want to toast some marshmallows, won't we?"

"I'll make you all some brownies, Allie baby,"

171

Mrs. Moore called from the kitchen. "You can count on me."

"Thanks, Mama," Allison called back. "Pete, your mother gave me that recipe, you know, the one you said you really liked."

"What can I make?" Hannah asked. "If Vonnie's bringing eggs and your mom's going to bake brownies . . ."

"I think that's enough stuff," Pete said. "Now who's going to help with the shopping?"

"Me," Hannah said. "When shall we do it?"

"How about right after school on Friday?" Pete asked. "Since the concert's that night Mr. Johnson's given me the afternoon off. I can go shopping with Hannah and we can put the stuff right in my car."

"Sorry," Hannah said. "I can't go shopping then. Got to report at the hospital."

"I can go then." Allison's whispery voice was so low Vonnie hardly heard her.

"Vonnie?" Pete asked.

"Sure, I can go along. How about it, Jeff? You want to come along too?"

"You've already got three people," Jeff said quietly. "How many does it take to buy a couple packs of dogs and buns, a couple cartons of soda?"

"Yeah," Pete said. "No need of us all going." He looked at his list thoughtfully for a moment, then Allison spoke up.

"Hey, we need tapes for your tape deck."

Pete added that to his list. "I'll bring the Bee Gees. You still like them?"

"You know it." Allison looked at Pete as if he were the only person in the room. "And do you still have those old Beatles tunes we used to play?"

Pete added Allison's suggestion to the list. "Unless someone thinks of something we've forgotten I guess that about does it."

"Yeah, that about does it all right," Hannah said.

Vonnie wondered if there was a double meaning to Hannah's words. She could almost feel sparks of anger flying between Allison and Jeff and she remembered a saying of her father's: Anger is just one letter away from danger. Was she imagining it or could she sense something special between Pete and Allison? Something dangerous? She wished she could stand up and shout that she thought the picnic was a terrible idea. But that wasn't the truth. The picnic was a good enough idea. It was Allison's presence she objected to.

Jealous. You're jealous. She tried to blot out her hurtful feelings, but she couldn't. She remembered Hannah's words: You're good therapy for Pete, Vonnie. Maybe Hannah was right. Maybe she was nothing more to Pete than therapy. Maybe Allison was the girl he really wanted to date. He seemed to know Allison's favorite foods and drinks and music. And they would make a handsome-looking couple. Then she remembered more of Hannah's words: You're the one who's wearing Pete's pin. She took a deep breath and made herself look at Allison.

"Thanks for having us over, Allison." Then she turned to Pete. "I hope you don't mind if we go now, Pete. I need to get home."

"You're not going to break up the party, are you, Pete?" Allison asked. "I mean, it's early yet."

"How about it, Vonnie?" Pete asked. "You really have to leave?"

"Yes. I really should." She was shaking inside. But Pete just smiled at her, then turned to Allison. "Guess we'll be going. See you tomorrow."

Had Pete hated leaving? Vonnie wished she knew. If he did he didn't say so. They talked about the picnic, about school, about everything except the way Allison had flirted with him. It was only when he kissed her goodnight that she felt she really didn't need to worry about Allison. Not tonight anyway.

16

On Thursday there was nothing in Pete's manner that suggested to Vonnie that he was interested in anyone except her. She had been wearing his pin night and day. She still hadn't told him about her health problem yet. Somehow she just couldn't find the right words. Maybe she was subconsciously waiting until after the picnic. And she knew that quite consciously she was hoping that after the picnic Allison would not be so visible in their lives.

Since all three boys were playing in the jazz concert, Vonnie, Hannah and Allison sat together in the auditorium's center section four rows from the front. They wore their dress jeans and all three of them had new shirts. Vonnie hadn't been surprised that Allison's shirt was green to match her shoes. Lots of the girls were wearing skirts to the concert, but Vonnie didn't let that bother her. Lots of girls weren't going on a picnic afterward.

She caught Pete's eye and he winked at her. All the band members wore dark slacks and gold jackets over white shirts and green ties, and their music stands were green with gold treble clef signs embossed in the center. She thought they looked as good as any professional band.

As the auditorium lights dimmed, voices hushed, the silvery spotlight focused on guest trombonist Bick Vane and Mr. Claribone tapped his foot to set a fast opening tempo. In the next moment Vonnie felt as if she were submerged in a vortex of sound. Brass. Reed. Percussion. The music rose in volume until her feet tingled from the vibration of the floor. Then as quickly as the sound had dominated the audience, it softened and mellow trombone tones flowed like honey soothing and lulling the senses.

"Isn't he neat?" Hannah whispered after the first number as she watched Bick Vane. "Tall. And I like long curly hair on a guy. And that black velvet suit—wow!"

"Yeah, Vonnie agreed. "He doesn't look too much older than we are either."

"I'm going to get his autograph afterward," Allison said. "Just think—we've heard him play on the *Tonight Show* and the *Today Show* and lots of other shows and we didn't even know it."

"Is it possible to be famous anonymously?" Hannah asked.

Before Vonnie could answer, the band began another tune and again they were held in the magic of tone and rhythm. Pete stood and played one chorus of a ballad and Jeff thumped out a piano solo in their third selection. The next to the last piece featured Chad on drums, and as the spotlight focused on him and his green and gold trap set Vonnie wondered if playing in the jazz band made up to him for being unable to go out for basketball. At times beating the drums and cymbals seemed more strenuous than dribbling a ball down a basketball court, but she supposed it really wasn't. She wished she could be as casual about her diabetes as Chad seemed to be about his rheumatic heart. She wondered how many other kids like herself had health problems that they never talked about. She really admired Chad's attitude. If only she were that strong! Well, she would tell Pete soon. Right after tonight's picnic she would have a long talk with him. She promised herself that.

After the concert ended the boys locked their instruments in the band room and changed into jeans, Allison got her autograph from Bick Vane, and they were ready to drive to Pete's farm for the picnic.

"Have we got everything?" Hannah asked.

"Don't be a worry wart," Chad said. "Let's go."

Jeff drove his car, taking Allison, Chad and Hannah, while Vonnie rode with Pete. The May night was soft and warm with just a hint of a south breeze that carried the scent of lilacs. Milky wisps of cloud lazed against the sable sky and the full moon was like an ivory ball suspended in nothingness. The roads were dry, and Pete opened wide steel gates so they could drive right across pasture land to the lake where willows grew at the shoreline, their fringed branches drooping toward their reflections in the black-mirror surface.

"Let's build a bonfire first," Pete called to the others as he and Vonnie jumped from the car. "It'll give us some light and a little warmth, too, in case anyone gets chilly."

"Nobody's going to get chilly," Allison said. "Let's go boating first."

"I say let's eat first," Jeff said. "I'm starving."

"So let's take a vote on it," Pete said.

Vonnie voted to eat first, and when building the bonfire and boating won out, she felt trapped. She had missed her evening snacktime and in the excitement of thinking about the concert and the picnic she had forgotten to slip some mints into her pocket. She needed to eat. She had only taken her regular shot of insulin, but she knew she had rushed at dinner. Maybe she could sneak part of a hot dog bun or a marshmallow without the others noticing. She walked back to the car. But no. The food was still locked in the trunk.

"Let Vonnie eat if she's so starved," Allison called out. "Pete, you can take *me* for a boat ride."

"No way," Pete said good-naturedly. "Jeff can teach you to row later. That's his job."

Vonnie felt her heart pounding. If she refused the boat ride Allison would surely take her place. She wasn't about to let that happen. She would be okay. She felt fine. She could grab something to eat the minute they got back.

Jeff gave Pete a hand with the red, flat-bottom boat, dragging it from where it was beached on the bank down to the water.

"Hop in, Vonnie," Pete invited. "We'll give it a test run to see that everything's okay."

"Have you ever been in a rowboat before?" Hannah asked her, joining them at the boat.

"Sure," Vonnie said. "Dad taught me how to row when I was in junior high."

"Then sit on the middle seat," Pete said. "I'll shove us off, then I'll join you and we can row across the lake and back just to see if she's going to float."

"And if she isn't?" Vonnie asked.

"I'm just kidding. Dad and I had her out yesterday for a trial run. She's sound."

"If you're afraid, I'll go," Allison said.

"I'm not afraid," Vonnie insisted. She wasn't

about to stay behind and let Allison float out on that shimmering moonlit water with Pete. But as she heard the bottom of the boat grate on shoreline rocks she felt troubled. On top of not eating enough, now she would be exercising, if she did her share of the rowing. And she could hardly refuse to row after she had bragged that she knew how.

"Ready?" Pete asked.

"Ready." She felt the smooth oak of the oar against her bare hands. "Let's go." She dipped her oar into the water and pulled. For a moment the boat started to turn in a circle, then Pete pulled on his oar and the bow pointed across the lake to the opposite shoreline.

"Shall we row across and back?" Pete asked.

"That's quite a ways, Pete. But . . . okay, if you really want to."

She had to pull hard on her oar to make her action match Pete's. She pulled and pulled and it was a few minutes before she could relax in the rhythm they established. She inhaled the sweet-pungent scent of the water. Waves splashed against the sides of the boat. The oars squeaked and squawked in the oar-locks. Then she heard a strange and beautiful sound that she didn't recognize. A birdcall. It was like the call she had heard the night she had gone to the library.

"What's that, Pete?" She paused in her rowing to listen and Pete paused too. For a moment they heard nothing but the shouts and laughter of the others as they built a bonfire on the shore. She was watching the red-orange flames lick into the dark night when the sound came again. At first it was a low trill, then a higher trill glissandoed into a warbling, clear call.

179

"Why, Vonnie, that's a mockingbird," Pete said. "Haven't you ever heard a mockingbird before?"

"I guess not. At least I don't recognize it."

"Maybe the sound coming across the water makes it seem different to you."

"It's such a sweet song, isn't it? And there's a sadness mixed with the sweetness."

"That's the mockingbird's true call," Pete said. "And it is pretty, but let's wait just a minute."

They sat silently for a few moments, then Vonnie looked at Pete in surprise and whispered, "I hear a cat."

"You hear the mockingbird imitating a cat," Pete said softly. "They're clever birds. They can imitate anything from a bawling calf to a squeaky hinge."

"But why would they want to imitate when their own song is so lovely?"

"Who knows!" Pete laughed. "I think they just like to play jokes on people. Listen! There's his own song again."

"It's so beautiful I wish I could record it and take it home with me," Vonnie said. Then she laughed.

"What's so funny?"

She laughed again. "I was just thinking that lots of couples have special songs that they call 'their song.' I guess our song will have to be a mockingbird's call."

"Don't laugh about it." Pete looked at her without smiling. "I like the idea. Anyone can claim a tune from a jukebox or a melody from a hit record as 'their song,' but we'll be unique. We'll remember the mockingbird's call, okay?"

"Hey, you guys!" Jeff shouted from the shore. "When you going to give someone else a turn?"

"We'd better get back to shore," Vonnie said. "I

really am hungry, Pete, and Jeff sounds half mad. The others are probably dying for a turn in the boat."

Vonnie let Pete pull on his oar until the bow pointed toward the blazing bonfire, then she began to row in rhythm with him. They had reached the shore and she was just stepping from the boat when she started feeling dizzy.

She felt in her pocket. No. She had forgotten her mints. "I need . . ." She tried to finish the sentence but her tongue felt fuzzy and her eyes wouldn't focus quite right. She sat down on the rocky shoreline as everything began to spin and go black.

"What's the matter, Vonnie?" Pete asked, leaning down toward her.

"Pete, I need some . . ." She tried to say: something sweet, but the words melted somewhere between her brain and her tongue. And then she didn't care any longer. The blackness around her was soft and warm and comforting.

17

The next time Vonnie wakened she sensed daylight against her closed eyelids. She moved her right hand slightly, feeling for the rocks that she remembered being beneath her, but her hand touched a smooth coolness. She inhaled the sharp scent of camphor and the smell of rubbing alcohol. With great effort she opened her eyes. Green walls. High bed. I.V. bottle and rack. Hospital. She was in a hospital bed. At first she thought she was alone in the room, then she heard a chair scrape against the floor, heard her mother's voice.

"Vonnie!"

"Mom?"

And her mother was at her side, leaning over her, peering at her, her eyes reddened from tears, her face tight and drawn.

"Oh, Vonnie! The doctor said you were going to be all right, but I just couldn't believe it until you opened your eyes, until you spoke to me. Let me get your father. He's waiting just outside the door in the corridor." Her mother left the room, then appeared again with her father.

"Vonnie!" Her father held her hand. "You've had a bad time, but it's all over now."

"What happened?" Vonnie asked, feeling as if she had just returned from a long journey in a strange place she couldn't quite remember.

"Don't you know?" her father asked.

She felt as if her head were swimming. Was she going to be sick? Then her stomach seemed to settle back into place. How could she feel so tired? All she wanted to do was sleep, but she made herself talk.

"We were at Pete's farm . . . at the lake. But that's all I can remember."

"Pete said you had been out in the rowboat and that when you got back to shore you passed out."

"Oh." Now she remembered. She hadn't eaten her snack. She had tried to ask Pete for something sweet. But where was Pete now?

"Vonnie," her mother said, "I hate to say I told you so, but if you hadn't told Pete about your diabetes you might not have survived this shock. Pete saved your life. He understood the problem and he rushed you to the emergency room and explained to the doctor, showed him your medical medallion, even before he called us."

If she hadn't told Pete! But she *hadn't* told him. She was sure she hadn't. She had tried to tell him there at the last minute, but it had been too late. She hadn't even been able to ask for something sweet. How had Pete known?

"Where's Pete now?"

"He went home right after we arrived," her father said. "How are you feeling now? I've signaled for the nurse."

How was she feeling? She wasn't sure. Weak. Tired. Confused. Mostly she was feeling confused. "I'm sorry I gave everyone a bad time." She glanced at the needle in her arm, then at the nurse who was coming through her doorway.

The nurse allowed them to talk for only a few moments, then urged Vonnie's parents to go home and get some sleep.

"You've been up all night long," the nurse said. "She'll be okay now. We want to keep her under observation for a day or so to be sure her insulin dosage is correct. You can come back and see her during visiting hours when you're rested."

"Maybe I should stay with her," her mother said. "I could nap right here in this chair."

"I'll be fine, Mom," Vonnie said. "You go on home with Dad and get some sleep. I'll see you later. I feel like sleeping myself. I'm so tired."

Reluctantly her parents left and the nurse gave her some pills and told her to try to sleep. She closed her eyes, but just pretended to sleep until the nurse left the room. She was tired, but she kept thinking of Pete. She needed to figure out some things. Had he known all along that she was diabetic? No, he couldn't have known. But he had told the doctor. Maybe he had just read it on her medallion. She had been wearing it around her neck. But no. Her shirt had been buttoned to her chin. He couldn't have seen the medallion.

At last she dozed, wakened, dozed again. And the next time she opened her eyes Hannah was in her room wearing her pink and white striped uniform. Vonnie grinned at her, realizing for the first time what a welcome sight a candy striper could be.

"Hannah! I'm glad you're here. And . . ."

"Are you feeling okay, Vonnie?"

"Yeah, I'm feeling okay, I guess. Has . . . has anyone called to ask about me?"

"Just your mother, Vonnie. She called once. I've just brought you some fresh water."

"Thanks."

Hannah looked directly at her. "Why didn't you tell anyone you had diabetes, Vonnie?"

"I . . . I . . . was afraid to, I guess."

"You should have been afraid *not* to tell."

"I didn't want to be . . . different. Surely you can understand that."

"I should have guessed. I should have guessed by the things you ate. Fine nurse I'll be if I don't sharpen up."

"What are the other kids saying about me now?"

"That you were dumb to try to keep a life or death matter a secret. Chad about flipped. He may really chew you out when you get back to school."

"I guess he'd have a right to. Chad of all people." She looked down at her sheets when she asked her next question. "Where's Pete, Hannah? Has he called?"

"Not yet. But don't worry, he will." Hannah headed for the door. "I'll see you later—before I go off duty. But I have to run now."

"Thanks for stopping in." She hated to see Hannah go, but she knew other patients needed her too. Where was Pete? Surely he didn't care anything about her. Surely Allison was the one he wanted to go out with. She knew from things her parents had said in the past that it was a scary thing to see a person go into insulin shock. If Pete cared anything about her he wouldn't have been able to go home to bed without even finding out how she was.

A nurse brought her a tray. She ate. She dozed. She slept. And the next time she opened her eyes Pete was standing at her bedside holding a small cassette player and a nurse was standing beside him. He had on the same jeans and red shirt he had worn on the picnic. How strange, she thought.

"Vonnie," the nurse said, "this boy says he thinks you'd like to see him. Is he right?"

"Yes." She smiled weakly, thinking that Pete had come for a duty visit. Maybe Allison was waiting outside in the corridor for him. Or outside in his car. Pete waited until the nurse left them before he took her hand and spoke.

"You scared me to death, you know it? I've been out of my gourd with worry."

"You don't have to pretend." Vonnie felt her throat tighten and begin to ache, but she was determined not to cry.

"What do you mean *pretend?*" Pete scowled. "I really was scared. If it hadn't been for Dianne . . ."

"What's Dianne got to do with it . . . with us?"

"My cousin's a diabetic, Vonnie. And she doesn't care who knows it. I'm going to have her talk to you about that sometime. But anyway, you act just the same way she acts about some things—about eating at school, for instance. She likes to eat at home. And she sneaks candy during class . . . with the teacher's permission, of course. And she wears a medical medallion around her neck."

"Then you knew all the time. . . ."

Pete shook his head. "I was just guessing. But when you passed out at the lake I felt sure that I had been right, so I checked to see if you were wearing that chain around your neck. I took one look at that medallion and brought you straight to the hospital."

She hid her hands under the sheet and clenched her fists. "How can I thank you, Pete?"

"Hey! No thanks necessary. I'm just pleased that I

did the right thing." Then his voice softened. "You mean a lot to me, Vonnie."

"Surely not so much." She turned her head away from him.

"Vonnie! Why do you say that?"

"I say it because it's true." She forced herself to look back at him again. "I know you and Allison . . . well, I know how it is."

"Allison and I will never be anything more than old friends. What's bothering you, Vonnie? Come on now. No more secrets."

Again she made herself meet his gaze. "Pete, if you really cared for me I don't think you could have gone home to bed without knowing how I was. I don't think. . . ."

"Hey! Wait just one darn minute." Pete's eyes snapped. "Who said anything about going home to bed?"

"My father said you went on home . . . and I . . . well, I guess I just assumed you went to bed."

"Well, you assumed wrong." Then his voice softened again. "Jeepers, Vonnie, if I'd known what you were thinking, I'd. . . . Sure I went home. I was in the way here. Nurses and doctors don't need extra people hanging around underfoot. But no way was I sleeping. I was thinking of you every minute. This will prove it."

Pete set the small cassette player he had been holding on the edge of her bed and turned it on. In a moment Vonnie heard the call of a mockingbird float into the room. She listened in silence until the tape stopped.

"You went back to the lake and recorded that mockingbird's song for me," Vonnie said. "Pete, I'm so sorry . . . I really thought . . ."

"Don't be sorry. Don't think. Just listen. It's our song, Vonnie, remember? *A special song for a special girl.* A special song for a special couple."

"Young man?" The nurse bustled back into the room. "I'm afraid I'll have to ask you to leave now. You can come back during regular visiting hours, of course."

Pete left the cassette player on her bedside table. " 'Bye, Vonnie. I'll be back later."

"Thanks, Pete. Thanks for . . . everything."

And he was gone. But she felt stronger already. The nurse said she wouldn't have to stay in the hospital long and the minute she got out she was going to tell the whole crowd what Pete had discovered on his own.

"Can I get something for you, Vonnie?" the nurse asked.

"Yes, please. On the shirt I was wearing when I came in there's a pin. I'd like to have it, please."

The nurse brought her the pin and Vonnie pinned it onto her hospital gown.

"It looks beautiful," the nurse said.

"I think so," Vonnie replied.

After the nurse left the room she turned on the cassette player, tuning the volume very soft as the sound of a mockingbird's call trilled into her room.

First Love from Silhouette

Two new titles are published on the first Friday of every month. All are available at your local bookshop, so make sure of obtaining your copies by taking note of the following dates:

JULY 1st

AUGUST 5th

SEPTEMBER 2nd

OCTOBER 7th

NOVEMBER 4th

DECEMBER 2nd

First Love from Silhouette

This Month's Titles

Songbird by Carrie Enfield

Tammy Hastings had never felt that she was especially good at anything. That was before Jeff Berger had asked her to sing with him on Talent Night. Overnight she became a star! Soon Jeff became the centre of her life. But she had to learn that you can't always command love—sometimes you just have to let it happen . . .

Special Girl by Dorothy Francis

There was something special between them, Pete Karmer told Vonnie Morrison. And that made moving to a new town easier. This time Vonnie was determined to be outgoing and friendly. But her determination to hide a part of her life caused misunderstandings and, worse yet, threatened to break up her first real romance.

First Love from Silhouette

Next Month's Titles

Please Love Me . . . Somebody by Maud Johnson

Julie Talbott acted so shy that some of her classmates had labelled her a snob. No one had guessed how much she wanted to start dating or that she had her eye on Eric Ford who sat opposite her in maths class. When Julie launched a campaign to get boys to notice her, she got some unexpected results. How could she have known that being popular could have its problems as well as its pleasures?

Love At First Sight by Elaine Harper

As the new girl in town Janine Anderson had no way of knowing that she had flipped over one of the most popular boys in school—Craig Matthews. When their part-time jobs brought Janine and Craig together, Janine's happiness knew no bounds. But being friends with Craig turned out to be more complicated than Janine had thought—especially when a jealous classmate stirred up rumours that threatened to come between them.

THERE'S NOTHING
QUITE AS SPECIAL AS A
FIRST LOVE.

85p each

1 ☐ NEW BOY IN TOWN
Dorothy Francis

2 ☐ GIRL IN THE ROUGH
Josephine Wunsch

3 ☐ PLEASE LET ME IN
Patti Beckman

4 ☐ SERENADE
Adrienne Marceau

5 ☐ FLOWERS FOR LISA
Veronica Ladd

6 ☐ KATE HERSELF
Helen Erskine

7 ☐ SONGBIRD
Carrie Enfield

8 ☐ SPECIAL GIRL
Dorothy Francis

All these books are available at your local bookshop or newsagent, or can be ordered direct from the publisher. Just tick the titles you want and fill in the form below.

Prices and availability subject to change without notice.

SILHOUETTE BOOKS, P.O. Box 11, Falmouth, Cornwall.

Please send cheque or postal order, and allow the following for postage and packing:

U.K. – 45p for one book, plus 20p for the second book, and 14p for each additional book ordered up to a £1.63 maximum.

B.F.P.O. and EIRE – 45p for the first book, plus 20p for the second book, and 14p per copy for the next 7 books, 8p per book thereafter.

OTHER OVERSEAS CUSTOMERS – 75p for the first book, plus 21p per copy for each additional book.

Name ....

Address ....

.. ..